St. Mary's High School Library
South Amboy, New Jersey

THE LAST OF ELLMAN

Also by James E. Nash

Poor Teddy Black

The Last of Ellman

JAMES E. NASH

HARPER & ROW, PUBLISHERS
New York, Evanston, San Francisco, London

1817

THE LAST OF ELLMAN. Copyright © 1971 by James E. Nash. All rights reserved. Printed in the United States of America. No part of this book may be used or reproduced in any manner whatsoever without written permission except in the case of brief quotations embodied in critical articles and reviews. For information address Harper & Row, Publishers, Inc., 49 East 33rd Street, New York, N.Y. 10016. Published simultaneously in Canada by Fitzhenry & Whiteside Limited, Toronto.

FIRST EDITION

STANDARD BOOK NUMBER: 06–013158–6

LIBRARY OF CONGRESS CATALOG CARD NUMBER: 72–156579

Designed by Yvette A. Vogel

For Kevin, Christopher, Christian and Shep

Part One

Chapter 1

"But he scares me," Mrs. Berger said. "He's by himself too much."

"Do you know how much time there is before the S.A.T. test?" Mr. Berger asked. "Less than three months. And if Marsh doesn't get a good score on that, then he won't make it into City College. And if he doesn't make it into City College, then he isn't going to college at all. And the way his grades are now, I can tell you he's not going to make it."

Mrs. Berger took her eyes from the television set and glared at her husband.

"It's only two subjects," she said. "So keep him in the house awhile and let him study."

"But he can't study by himself. Don't you understand that? He needs somebody to help him."

"For *history?*" Mrs. Berger asked scornfully. "For English? In science maybe I could see it, but in the kind of subjects Marsh has trouble with, all you have to do is read and memorize. For that you don't need a teacher."

"Marsh does and his grades prove it."

"So all right! But get him a teacher! Don't go to some nut just because he has a lot of books and lives in the same house."

"Who told you Mr. Ellman is a nut?"

"Nobody had to tell me. I can see it for myself. Watch him

3

sometime when he's walking along the street. He talks to himself. I don't want Marsh getting mixed up with people like that."

Mrs. Berger returned to the television set, seeking to nestle herself in the warm burrow of a murder story, but she was held off by the cold, wet hands of a laundry commercial.

"Number one," said Mr. Berger, resuming his attack. "Did you ever talk to him? Did you ever in your life so much as say hello to him?"

Mrs. Berger was not perturbed. "I say hello to everybody at least once," she said. "I wouldn't keep it up with *him*, though, because I'd be afraid he'd say hello back to me."

"Well, I *have* talked to him. A good many times. And I know he's a very interesting and intelligent man."

Mr. Berger felt no compulsion to remind his wife that most of his conversations with Ellman had been limited to the subject of whether or not Ellman's overflowing bathtub was the cause of the leak in the Bergers' bathroom. Every time they developed a leak in their bathroom, Mrs. Berger sent Mr. Berger upstairs to make sure Ellman's tub was not overflowing. And Ellman always led him through a cluttered apartment to show him a bone-dry bathtub.

"It's probably one of the pipes," Ellman would say. "These old buildings . . ."

"I know," Mr. Berger would answer. "I just thought I'd check it out anyway. You never can tell."

Only once had Mr. Berger had anything like a real conversation with Ellman. He'd been sitting out on the front stoop one evening during the previous summer when Ellman came along the street. The boys playing around the hydrant at the corner had splashed water on him and the old man's trousers were dripping. Mr. Berger started to sympathize with him, but Ellman had dismissed it and joined Mr. Berger on the stoop. They had sat there for an hour together, discussing childhood on the sidewalks and warmly remembering their own days of dancing under the hydrants.

"It's not the children we should blame," Ellman had said. "It's the big fellow with the wrench. Here we are with a water shortage on our hands and he tells the children that it is no concern of theirs. *They* will somehow take care of it. And when *they* finally do show up—in the form of the police—he hides the wrench in the hallway and comes back out to lead the kids in jeering and razzing the cops while they turn off the pump. That makes him a hero, someone the kids look up to and admire."

Mr. Berger's silence was beginning to interfere with his wife's concentration.

"You didn't talk to him about Marsh, did you?" she asked.

"I didn't yet, but I'm going to."

"Listen, I'm not raising any eccentrics in this house."

"What are you talking about—*eccentrics?*"

"You send Marsh up to that man and pretty soon Marsh'll be just the way he is—holding long talks with himself while the whole street laughs at him."

"Well, if that's what it comes to," Mr. Berger said, "then that's the way it'll be."

"Oh, it's settled, is it?" she said sarcastically. "Thanks for telling me."

"No, it's not settled," he answered. "Tomorrow when I come home from work I'm going to talk to Marsh. If he agrees to give Ellman a chance, I'll go upstairs tomorrow night and have a talk with him. *Then* it'll be settled."

Mr. Berger was just unwrapping a corned beef sandwich when Gene Quinn came over to the shipping desk to join him for lunch. Gene, at thirty-two, was a shop supervisor. He had a wife, two kids and a half dozen prematurely gray hairs.

"You heard the latest?" he asked. "They say the company may move out of town."

"Who says?" Mr. Berger asked.

"The rumor is going around. They say that's why they hired Sweety-Face. He's supposed to coordinate the move."

"Sweety-Face" was the twenty-two-year-old new man in the front office. Although he had been with the company for less than three months, he drew a salary greater than either Phil Berger's or Gene Quinn's but nobody in the shop had been able to figure out what his duties were.

"They can't move!" Mr. Berger said. "It's in the union contract."

"Then what's Sweety-Face doing?"

"How should *I* know? Every time I go into the office I see him sitting there with his feet on the desk talking into the telephone. Maybe he's a salesman."

"That's a salesman?" Gene said.

One of Mr. Berger's messengers returned. It was Lanny, a tall, long-haired kid with a grudge against the world.

"You want to take lunch now or go out on your next trip and take it while you're out?" Mr. Berger asked.

Lanny looked at Mr. Berger as if it was a dumb question.

"Just give me the tickets," he said.

"Okay," Mr. Berger said. "I was just asking."

Mr. Berger consulted a clipboard. He handed Lanny four pickup slips, two delivery receipts and two subway tokens, consulted his watch and began to sign him out.

"The packages are on the bottom shelf," Mr. Berger said.

Lanny collected his packages and studied his receipts.

"I need another token," he said.

"What for?" Mr. Berger asked. "You got one for uptown and one for down. What else do you need?"

"One of these is Thirty-ninth and Broadway. The other is Fortieth and Madison. I don't have to walk across town like that. I need bus fare."

"Bus fare?" Mr. Berger said. "It's only three blocks."

"Three blocks midtown carrying packages? I don't have to walk that. I got a right to bus fare."

Gene interrupted the conversation with a laugh.

"If he gives you the bus fare, you'll probably walk it anyway and put the money in your pocket," he said knowingly.

"What business is that of yours?" Lanny said. "I don't have to put up with anything from you. I don't work in your department."

Mr. Berger gave him the bus fare and got rid of him.

"Damn kids!" he said. "You'd think they were doing you a favor working."

Mr. Berger went back to his sandwich. He tried to get more details about the proposed move, but Gene kept switching the conversation to the subject of Sweety-Face.

"You really hate that guy, don't you?" Mr. Berger said.

"I don't hate him. It's just he's nothing. Four-year college man, so he gets to walk around in a suit and do nothing all day."

"Hey, that's right, you had two years of college, didn't you?"

Mr. Berger had hit on Gene's sore spot.

"It was a waste of a good two years," Gene said. "I'd have been better off with no college at all. You tell people you didn't go to college and they let it go at that. Tell them you had two years of college and right away they start asking why you didn't finish."

"Still and all," Mr. Berger said. "The more education you got, the better your chances of getting a good job."

"Bull," Gene said. "It's all or nothing. Look at me. Ten years with this company and I'm still working in a T-shirt. Sweety-Face has been here two months and he hasn't even got his hands dirty yet."

"Marsh is trying to get into City College now," Mr. Berger said.

"City College? He shouldn't have any trouble getting in.

7

They're on open admissions now, aren't they? Taking in anybody that wants to go."

"No. They may start that next year but, even if they do, it'd be too late for Marsh."

"When does he graduate?" Gene asked.

"This June."

"It's January now, he's graduating in June, and he's still not signed up? You better tell him to hustle it, boy. He's got a real problem."

"He's gonna take the Scholastic Aptitude Test in March," Mr. Berger said. "We're thinking of getting a tutor to help him get ready for it."

Gene expressed a polite interest in the idea. Mr. Berger told him as much as he knew about the old man upstairs.

"What does he do for a living?" Gene asked.

"Nothing," Mr. Berger answered. "He's retired."

"Well, what did he do before?"

"He used to work at the post office."

"He was a mailman?" Gene asked incredulously.

Mr. Berger saw his portrait of the Big Brain Upstairs turning into a cartoon.

"Not a mailman," he said scornfully. "He used to work in the main office. He was in charge of regulations or something like that. *Mailman!*"

Gene shrugged. "Well, what do I know about it?" he said defensively.

Gene asked if Mr. Berger was going to pay the old man for his services.

"Pay him!" Mr. Berger said. "Where would I get any money to pay him? Besides, he doesn't need it. He's got more money than I ever dreamed of."

"From the post office?"

"He's got a good pension," Mr. Berger asserted. "Besides, he had wealthy relatives."

Gene crumpled up the sandwich wrappings and threw them into a nearby trashcan.

"He had wealthy relatives, so he took a job at the post office," he said sarcastically.

"His brother died a few years ago and left him some money. He's got a nephew in Wall Street and another nephew who's an accountant. They take care of the money for him. All right, maybe he's not rich or anything like that, but he's comfortable."

"Okay," Gene said. "So you don't have to pay him. That's all I wanted to know."

"He'd probably be insulted if I offered him money," Mr. Berger said. "I bet he'd throw me out of the house."

Gene had some doubts on that point, but Mr. Berger overrode them.

"I been around," he said, nodding his head. "I know what it's like. And most of the time I'd agree with you: The money is the thing. But in something like this, no."

"The money is always the thing," Gene said. "What do you think got Sweety-Face where he is today? His folks had money."

"Education," Mr. Berger said. "That's what got it for him. I have a friend, Bill Grady. I used to work with him when I had that part-time job going. Well, his son just got out of college last spring. Last spring, I said. And that kid is making more today than his father does after twenty-two years on the same job."

"Well, that's what I was saying. . . ."

"Accounting," Mr. Berger continued. "That's what he went in for. And even before he got out of college he was being interviewed for jobs. He went to four interviews and at each one they offered him a job. He was all set before he even left college. Went straight from school to the job. And do you know what kind of a salary he's making at that job?"

Mr. Berger paused while Gene shrugged.

"Listen to this," Mr. Berger said. "He started that job at two hundred and fifty dollars a week. Started! And that's not saying anything about the benefits, the credit cards, the expense accounts and the company car."

Gene said nothing. He was lost in reflections on the two more years it would have taken him to get his degree.

"And don't get me wrong," Mr. Berger said. "This kid is no Einstein, either. He's just a regular guy like you and me. Only that's what college can do for you. You could be the stupidest guy in the world and still start out miles ahead of the rest of us. All you need is that little piece of paper that says 'I went to college.'"

Mr. Berger was silent for a minute. Then he turned and pointed his finger in the direction of the front office.

"And that's what Marsh is going to have," he said.

At two o'clock, Julius Ellman asked his nephew to drive him to the railroad station.

"No need for that," Norman explained. "I'm going to take you home myself as soon as these people leave."

"I'd rather go now by train," Ellman said. "I really came only for the funeral and I'm beginning to get a headache."

"If that's the way you want it," Norman said. "Just let me tell Karen."

Ellman's sister-in-law, Ida, had died only two months after her first grandchild was born. From the cemetery most of the mourners had driven to Norman's home on Long Island to get their first glimpse of the baby, with the result that most of the conversation had been concerned with maternity benefits and baby care. Ellman was relieved when he and Norman finally found themselves in the car on the way to the station.

"What did you think of the baby?" Norman asked.

"He's beautiful, of course," Ellman said.

There was something defensive in Norman's voice. Ellman glanced over at him. Norman's expression was merely that of a careful driver keeping his eyes on the road.

"It must seem strange to you," Norman said. "Our showing the baby off and all at a time like this. But a lot of those people are from the city. I work with them on the job and they don't get out this way often. This will probably be the only chance most of them ever get to see him."

"I don't think it's strange at all, Norman," Ellman said. "I was delighted myself to have a chance to see the baby."

"It's appropriate, in a way," Norman said. "Mom was always after us to give her a grandchild. It shows she left something behind. It ensures the continuity of the family."

Ellman knew that the continuity of the family meant even less to Norman than it meant to Ellman himself, but he avoided flinching at the words. In a way, Ellman admired Norman for the unabashed bluntness with which he brought forth his platitudes. It made him so vulnerable that one either had to bludgeon him to death or pretend to respect his sentiments.

They stopped at an intersection.

"People don't make such a fuss about these things nowadays," Norman said.

For a moment Ellman was not sure whether it was the bereaved son or the proud father talking. He looked at Norman again to make sure. Norman was staring intently at the traffic light.

"She was old," Ellman said. "Toward the end she was in great pain. The last time I saw her she was *wishing* for death."

The light changed and they drove on.

"The important thing to remember," Norman said, "is that life goes on."

There's flattery in that, Ellman thought. I'm in my sixties and retired and he feels no need for delicacy in describing the ease with which the dead can be put out of mind.

When they got to the station, Norman insisted on waiting with Ellman until the train came. He filled the time by giving him financial advice and warning him not to get involved in any get-rich-quick schemes.

Ellman smiled. It was a running joke between them. Norman knew perfectly well that Ellman made a point of living on his pension and that the few thousand dollars his brother Jacob had left him was little more to him than a toy for his nephews to play at investing with. Still, they were careful players and the money had more than tripled in the eight years since Jacob's death.

As the train pulled in, Norman began urging Ellman to come out and visit them again soon.

"Don't wait until income tax time," he said. "Come out and visit us often. Remember, we *are* your family."

Ellman smiled, got on the train and waved good-bye.

He took a seat near a window in the middle of the car. Only after the conductor had taken his ticket and the train was well on its way did he begin to relax and feel like himself again.

It was a regrettable fact, but a fact nonetheless, that Ellman simply could not talk to his real nephews while they were present. Once he was safely on the train going back to Manhattan, however, he was free to hold a long conversation with his dream nephews.

Now he was Ellman, a man of substance and strength, a man whose learning and accomplishments were well known, and whose words commanded respect. This was the Ellman who could announce that "A funeral is a time to talk about the past," and who would talk about it even if his only audience was an imaginary one. Especially if his audience was an imaginary one. Because with no one to contradict him, no one to raise an eyebrow or ask a question, Ellman could be as eloquent as he pleased.

And if the well-dressed matron across the aisle cast an uneasy glance at him every now and then, all that meant was that he would have to curb his lip movements a little.

Yes, a funeral was a time to think of the past. But although it had been Ida's funeral, it was not Ida's past that Ellman thought of. Ida had always been something of a shadowy figure, even in the last few months when he had visited her in the hospital. She had deserved attention and respect because she was Jacob's widow, but she had outlived Jacob by eight years and now that she too had died, the shadow had been removed. It was his brother Jacob that Ellman thought of now. Jacob as he had been while they grew up together.

Ellman had no sentimental attachment to the old days of the lower East Side. They were hard days and bitter ones. But the one thing he could say for them was that in those days there was such a thing as family. It was not something that was planned or talked about or even sentimentalized about. It just *was* and you knew it.

What a family they had been! Papa, the pillar of strength, Mama, the Tower of Babel, and the two boys, Julius and Jacob.

Jacob had said to Ellman after his second son was born, "Look, now I have two boys. Just like us."

"No," Ellman said aloud. "They were not like us."

The woman across the aisle removed her ticket stub from the notch in front of her and moved to the back of the car. Ellman pressed his lips together and gazed out the window until the gentle monotony of the ride lulled him back into his reverie.

Ellman's father had been a scholar, a teacher. From him Ellman had inherited his love of books and learning. But his mother had not encouraged that love. Books were fine things, she said, and she was second to none in her respect for wisdom. But what good had learning ever done his father? Books were a luxury for those who had leisure. First learn a trade. Then earn the leisure. Then enjoy the books.

His father might have achieved greater affluence if he had not been both an atheist and an anarchist. Ellman could still remember the arguments his father had had with neighbors in the street.

"The fool saith in his heart 'There is no God,'" someone would quote at him.

"Correct!" the old man would reply. "The fool says in his heart there is no God. And the wise man says it out loud for all the world to hear. There is *no God.*"

Ellman had always been a little ashamed of his father's atheism. Most of the time people assumed that Julius Ellman was every bit as Jewish as he looked and sounded. But, whenever anyone came down to the point of asking about his background, Ellman always described himself as being only half Jewish. It was a gesture of grudging respect for his father, who, in attempting to free himself from the limitations of a tradition he felt he had outgrown, had succeeded only in cutting off his children from its benefits.

In 1917, when Ellman was twelve years old, his father left the house one evening to attend a meeting at the home of his friend Melnick the tailor, who was sometimes known as Melnick the bomb-maker. One of Melnick's home-made explosives went off that night, killing Melnick and seriously injuring two of his comrades.

Ellman could still remember the pounding on the door that night and the fear in his mother's eyes as she told him that she had to go out and that he must stay home and look after Jacob, who was then only six.

Within one week of that fatal meeting, Ellman was forced to leave school and take a job in a meat market at the other end of town. It was months before he saw his father again. When they finally did bring him home, he was no longer the father Ellman remembered but a bitter, blind old man who sat in a corner all the time, refusing to speak.

Even Mr. Nonsch could not make him speak, although his fiddle-playing was the only thing that was known to bring a smile to his scarred face. Nonsch the fiddler had long been a friend of the family and, after their father's accident, he came to visit them almost every day. Of course, he took some interest in both of the boys, but it was Jacob who interested him most. It was Jacob for whom the fiddler used to play and, although Julius dearly loved music, it was Jacob to whom Mr. Nonsch offered to give music lessons. Julius, at twelve years of age, was now the main support of the family and had to be considered a man.

One hot summer day, when there was no one in the house but himself and young Jacob, the blind man climbed out onto the windowsill and tumbled down to the sidewalk three stories below. Mrs. Gerlich across the street witnessed the accident.

"I guess he just wanted to climb out on the fire escape to get a breath of air," she said. "Only he must have climbed out the wrong window by mistake. The poor man."

It was years before Ellman had any second thought on the subject.

"How did we live through such times?" Ellman asked. It was a rhetorical question aimed at his imaginary nephews, but it was answered with a humorous smile by a conductor on the Long Island Railroad.

Ellman closed his eyes. What difference did it make what people thought?

Ellman worked, his mother worked, and Jacob went to school. Grammar school, high school, music school. Mr. Nonsch faded out of the picture and Ellman found a job in the evening to pay for the music lessons. This meant deferring indefinitely his hope of continuing his own education in night school, but then that could wait. Meanwhile, he studied what he could from Jacob's books and, every day, he made Jacob tell him as much as he could remember of what went on in class.

It was Jacob on whom all attention settled. The shining Jacob, who was to be a musical genius. Jacob played the violin and the house revolved around him. To Julius and the family, to the uncles and aunts who drifted back into his life after his father's death, and to everyone who knew them, Jacob's playing was beautiful. No wedding was complete, no bar mitzvah was official, no party was successful without Jacob there to play his fiddle.

But to the rest of the world Jacob was just another violinist. For years, while he was still going to school in the mornings, he played in the pit in theaters on Second Avenue. Once he played as a substitute with the NBC Symphony. Then, for a long time, he was with the Contradini Orchestra, playing lush arrangements of show tunes.

Each year he would come back to the old Saltzman Music School to play in the Alumni Concert. There he was a star, featured in the third movement of Tchaikovsky's Violin Concerto. At one such concert, after Jacob had done his piece and while most of the audience was applauding and shouting "Bravo," a student in front of Ellman turned to the girl with him and said, "No wonder nobody ever heard of him." That casual comment, uttered so long ago, still troubled Ellman. Jacob was no Heifetz, perhaps, but he was a good violinist, capable of giving great pleasure to anyone who had the good sense to relax and enjoy himself. Wasn't that enough? True, Jacob had not achieved fame or fortune, but he had raised and educated two sons and provided a comfortable home for them and their mother.

"Jacob *was* a success," Ellman said aloud. Then he remembered where he was and opened his eyes. Nobody in the train was paying attention to him now.

Jacob was a success, because Jacob had been a wonderful human being.

But to make Jacob a success Ellman had had to forget forever his dream of returning to school. Instead he hauled scrap in a junkyard, pushed racks through the garment district and, through an acquaintance of Jacob's, finally obtained a steady position in the post office.

The post office had seemed like a refuge when he first went into it. The country was in the midst of the Depression and, if nothing else, the post office offered security. For the rest, Ellman's life was his own dead dreams and his scrapbook on Jacob.

Ellman had met his wife, Ruth, at one of the old music school recitals. She was learning the piano. Recitals were informal affairs then, held every Monday night, with coffee and cake served after the music at a cost of twenty-five cents per person. He and Ruth had been married for only a year when she died. The only reminders of her now were the upright piano in the corner of Ellman's apartment and the picture over it, showing him and Ruth on their wedding day. They had had no children and Ellman had never wished to marry again.

Instead he surrounded himself with books. At first they were novels about ambitious young men and they fired his own ambition. But when he tried to work it off at his job, he failed time and time again because it simply would not take root there. His heart still lay in the daydream that should have died the day his father was blinded, the dream of becoming a teacher, a guide to the young as he had been to his brother Jacob and as he would have been to his own children if he had had any.

"Pennsylvania Station next," the conductor called sharply.

Ellman checked his watch. It was still early afternoon, so he decided to go down and browse among the secondhand bookshops on Fourth Avenue before going home.

Chapter 2

The parcel containing his new book sat on the counter in front of him while Ellman forced down a meal that seemed well-nigh indigestible—a charcoal-charred steak, steaming, soggy french fries and a salad so green that it looked every bit as artificial as it tasted.

Ellman had long since accustomed himself to swallowing bad food in the interest of nourishment but what he could never get used to was people like the two ladies on his left who kept telling one another what a nice place this was and how tasty the food was. He glanced over at the counter in front of them several times to make sure they were having the same "special" he had, and it was all he could do to keep from making rude remarks to them, so much did their plastic eulogies grate on him.

He forced down the last morsel, left a quarter tip on the counter and carried his parcel off to the corner of the street, where he waited ten minutes for the bus to come along. Once in the bus, however, he could not resist the temptation of the brown parcel. He struggled for a moment with the bit of plastic tape that held the wrapping together and then slipped the book out.

Ten Ways to Analyze Your Mind, by Carlton Dexter. The title was printed in white and gray on a yellow background, the letters shaped to look as though they had been carved out of a wall. Carefully Ellman took the jacket off the book and set it in his lap under the brown paper.

He was slightly embarrassed by the title. How absurd, people would think, a man his age reading books on self-improvement. There would be no chance for him to explain to them that it was not himself he was trying to analyze at all.

He opened the book, scanned the table of contents and began to read the preface.

The ten ways to analyze one's mind were through one's Memories, Interests, Knowledge, Imagination, Intuition, Skills, Habits, People (Emotions), Beliefs and Contradictions.

"It is absurd, of course," said Ellman. "But then there is always the germ of an idea, the hint of a truth."

The preface explained in brief terms what each of the steps involved. The chapter on Intuition was apparently going to deal with extrasensory perception. Ellman raised his eyes from the book to dwell for a moment on the sheer gall of its author and noticed that the bus was just pulling into his stop. He rose quickly and moved to the exit door at the back.

"Hey, mister!" cried a voice behind him.

He was climbing down into the street when a young man grabbed his arm.

"You dropped this," the young man said.

It was the brown wrapping paper and the glaring dust jacket. The young man was holding the jacket by a corner as if he wanted to be sure that everyone had an opportunity to read the embarrassing title. Ellman snatched it out of his hand so suddenly that the corner tore off and remained between the young man's fingers.

"Idiot!" Ellman snapped, as the door closed behind him. "Thank you."

As the bus pulled away, he rolled the cover up hastily,

stuffed it into his coat pocket and set off on the two-block walk to his home.

While she was over at Mrs. Ferling's that afternoon, Mrs. Berger had promised to lend her a blue purse to use at her niece's wedding. But now, at home Mrs. Berger had no idea where the blue purse was.

She had been absolutely certain when she came in that it was in the top drawer of the bedroom bureau, but now the entire contents of the bureau had been turned out and the purse was nowhere in sight.

On the shelf in the closet, she thought.

She dragged a chair from the kitchen and climbed up on it to reach the shelf. Lots of paper bags, the box Mr. Berger kept his old income tax papers in, a few of Marsh's old schoolbooks, but no purse.

She went over every inch of closet space and through every drawer in the house. Time and again she slapped herself on the forehead and said, "Of course! I know where it is!" And still she did not find it. A hundred times in the course of the search she felt she was right on the brink of discovery and actually found herself acting out the way she would explain it to Mrs. Ferling.

"I was just about to give up when suddenly I moved this big shopping bag that I keep my old shoes in and right behind it . . ."

The purse was not behind it.

"I went through that drawer three times and I could have sworn in court that the purse wasn't there. But then I said to myself, 'One more time. It can't hurt to have one more look.' And wouldn't you know . . ."

The purse was not there the fourth time, either.

Several times she abandoned the search completely, but even that was only a way of trying to make the charm work.

"I decided to give it up as a bad job. I said to myself the purse is lost, that's all there is to it. You may as well flop out in front of the television and watch your stories. So that's what I did. And just like that, during one of the commercials, I happened to glance over at this shelf in the corner where I keep a lot of knickknacks and odds and ends and would you believe it . . ."

The purse was not there, either.

Her last hope was that Mr. Berger or Marsh might have seen it and put it somewhere.

Marsh was usually home by three o'clock. She would ask him as soon as he arrived. Meanwhile, she was free to enjoy her stories. But every once in a while, during the commercials, she resumed her explanation to Mrs. Ferling.

"I really didn't think Marsh would put it anyplace. It was just a last resort that I asked him. Because he knows better than to touch my things. I told him about that a thousand times. But he just walked across the room and picked it up. It was right under my nose all the time. He says to me, 'Mom, you put it right there yourself the other day. I *saw* you.'"

At four o'clock, the last of what Mrs. Berger called the "good stories" went off the air. It was four-thirty before she heard a click at the door and a cautious "I'm home," announcing Marsh's arrival.

"Where have you been all this time?"

"I had to go uptown for something."

"Uptown for what? Did you see my blue purse?"

"I went to buy tickets for a show. What blue purse?"

"The one I used to keep in my bureau drawer—with the silver clasp on it."

"Maybe you threw it out."

The suggestion that she might throw out anything so precious as the blue purse indicated to Mrs. Berger that Marsh was going to be no help to her at all. She watched him as he lazily dumped his books and sneakers into the bottom of his closet.

"I have to go out again," he announced.

"Go out?" she said. "You just got in."

"I have to see Donna at her job to tell her I got the tickets and give them to her to hold."

"What tickets?"

"For the show."

"So what's this big show you gotta buy tickets for ahead of time? When are you going? Tonight?"

"A couple of weeks from now. On a Thursday."

"So what did you buy the tickets today for?"

"You have to buy the tickets ahead of time. That's the way they work it. It's not a regular show. It's a . . . Broadway play."

Marsh had never been to a Broadway play before and he hoped for a moment that his mother would restore his sense of his own sophistication by asking him if he couldn't wait until they brought it downtown or until they showed it on television. Instead she only shrugged.

"I felt real stupid," Marsh said. "She asked me to get the cheapest seats in the balcony, so I walked right up to the window and asked this guy to give me just that, the cheapest seats. They have a big diagram in the lobby so you can see where you're going to sit. We sit in the last row, as high up and as far back as you can get."

"What's the name of the show?"

"*Adamant Eve.*"

Mrs. Berger looked uneasy, as if Marsh had let slip in her presence one of the obscenities she felt sure he must use among his friends.

"*Adam and Eve?*" she repeated.

"*Adamant,*" Marsh said. He spelled it for her. "I don't know what it means, but it's a comedy and it's supposed to be funny. It's got that guy in it that you see on the Ed Sullivan show—Alan Horgan. He's good."

"Oh, you're gonna see him in person, you mean?"

"Something like that."

Marsh was nearly at the door when she asked him what time he was coming back. To Marsh it seemed that he was always nearly at the door when she asked him what time he was coming back.

"About six," he said. "In time for supper."

"Good. You going out again after supper?"

"No. I got a lot of homework I have to do. That's why I want to go to Donna now."

"That reminds me," his mother said. "Come inside. I want to talk to you for a minute."

If Marsh had not mentioned the word "homework," Mrs. Berger thought, it would never have occurred to her to attempt to influence him against his father's project. But since, in a sense, it was Marsh himself who had brought it up, she had no qualms about expressing her opinion on the subject.

Marsh stepped back into the apartment and closed the door behind him. He did not close it all the way, however. His mother stood there waiting for the sound of the clicking latch to assure her that she had Marsh's full attention. The sound did not come.

"I'm in kind of a hurry," Marsh said.

"It's just this," his mother said. "I had a talk with your father last night about this college business and everything, and he's going to have a talk with you tonight. He's got some stupid idea about getting a private teacher for you."

"The old man upstairs, you mean," Marsh said.

Mrs. Berger had been outmaneuvered. "So he *did* tell you about it," Mrs. Berger said. "And he swore to me he didn't."

"Well, he didn't talk to me about it exactly," Marsh said. "I guessed, in a way. We were talking about the low marks I got in English and history last term and I told Dad that the guidance counselor said that the only way I could get into City College is by getting a high score on my Scholastic Aptitude

23

Test. I kept trying to explain how they figure your school average against your test mark to come up with a composite score and all the time Dad kept mentioning this old guy upstairs and how smart he was. I kind of figured what he was getting at."

"That's your father, all right. Everybody can see through him."

"Anyway, what did he say?"

"Only that he was going to talk to you."

"No. I mean what did the old man say?"

"Oh, he didn't get that far yet. He hasn't talked to the old man. At least, that's what he told me. If you want to believe that."

Mrs. Berger softened her tone.

"Listen, Marsh, you don't really want to go up to him for a teacher, do you? It's not as though he was a member of the family or anything like that. For all you know he could be a crazy strange old man."

Marsh frowned.

"I'll hear what Dad has to say," he said. "We'll talk it over tonight and see then."

After Marsh had left, Mrs. Berger saw exactly what tack she should have taken.

I should have made Marsh just stay in the house and study.

What was all this business about a tutor anyway? Who needed one? She or his father could give Marsh all the help he needed. Any one of his friends from school could have done it. One person reads questions from the book and the other one answers them. That's all there is to it. And if you don't know the answer, the other one gives it to you and you keep repeating it over and over until you do know it. What was so hard about that?

She was working herself up into an angry fit when she suddenly remembered that she had lent her blue purse to her sister two weeks ago. She picked up the phone and began dialing her sister's number.

After the preface on "How to Use This Book," there was a chapter called "Why Analyze Your Mind?" (because it was the key to fame and fortune); then ten chapters, one devoted to each of the different analytical approaches; and, finally, a chapter called "The Rest Is up to You," in which the reader was sent forth into the world presumably armed with an arsenal of self-knowledge. Ellman was very familiar with the pattern by now, having read a whole library of such books. Not, indeed, that he really needed to analyze himself ten ways. He did not want to triple his reading speed, either, or develop a dynamic personality or an infallible memory, and yet his bookshelves were full of volumes on these subjects. The truth was that he was fascinated by the possibilities of the mind and that each of these books had some little germ of truth in it that he wished to understand. Of course, he would admit, only the very naïve would swallow them whole. And yet he could not help believing that if he had had in the days of his youth the same insights which these books had provided him in his age, the whole course of his life might very easily have been changed.

Besides . . . to read such books and to imagine the kind of mind that could be excited and inspired by them—it was like returning for a while to an earlier and simpler age. If such books needed a justification, then perhaps the best he could give was that he found them more interesting than novels.

He was well into the chapter on Intuition when there came a knock at the door.

As was his habit whenever anything roused him from his concentration, Ellman looked first at the clock. It was nine-thirty, two hours since he had sat down with the book. He was musing on what a diverting two hours it had been when the knock came a second time.

Ellman sighed and went to answer it. The sight of a familiar face at the door caused him a slight shock.

"I'm sorry I kept you waiting," he said. "I've gotten to the point where I don't even listen to the door anymore. When I do hear it, it's always either someone selling something, or a delivery boy who's got the wrong apartment."

Mr. Berger seemed to be hesitating over something.

"It's not the bathroom again, is it?" Ellman asked.

"No," said Mr. Berger, smiling. "No more leaks."

Mr. Berger put his hand on the door, as though he were afraid Ellman might close it in his face.

"Can I come in for a minute?" he said. "There's something I'd like to talk to you about."

"Of course," said Ellman, stretching his arm out to open the door as wide as possible. "Come right in."

He led Mr. Berger into the living room.

"I don't really *collect* newspapers," he said, clearing a stack of them from one of the chairs. "But I clip things out of them. Sometimes I fall behind and they accumulate."

Ellman had nothing but tea or coffee to offer his guest and Mr. Berger declined both. Ellman took a chair and they sat across the table from each other.

"If I'd have gone to college," Mr. Berger began abruptly, "I would have become a designer. I never told this to anyone before, but that's the one thing I always wanted to do. When I was a kid I used to like drawing pictures of cars and airplanes and things like that, and I always hoped that when I grew up I'd be able to design new cars and things."

Mr. Berger paused and stared silently at the table.

"Not that I'm complaining," he continued. "I don't really have a bad life, and there's no point in looking back into the past, is there? Only now I *have* got a problem. My son, Marsh. You've probably seen him around."

"I know the boy," said Ellman.

"He wants to become an engineer. He's got his heart set on it. Only, to make an engineer out of him, it takes a hell of a lot of money. Of course, my wife and I always planned for him to go to college. When he was little we even had a college fund for him. We didn't put very much into it, but they were regular, steady deposits. But my mother's last illness ate up most of it."

Mr. Berger paused and lost himself in reflection. Ellman, uncertain where all this was leading, did not say anything.

"Oh, don't worry," Mr. Berger resumed. "I'm not building up to a touch. We figure we can see the kid through if only he can get himself into one of the free city colleges."

"I see," said Ellman.

"The trouble is that it's not as easy to get into those colleges as it looks. They only have room for so many students. Naturally, they take the ones with the highest averages. Now I'm not saying Marsh isn't a good student. In things like mathematics and science his grades are fine. His trouble comes with the humanities. That's where he needs help."

At precisely this moment, a door opened at the back of Ellman's mind and a long dormant Julius Ellman began groping his way toward the light.

"Mr. Berger," he said. "Are you asking me to give lessons to your son?"

"If it was anything like mathematics or science, that's constantly changing every day, I'd never dream of mentioning it. But it's the humanities and you're an educated man."

"Just what area is your son having most difficulty with?"

"The whole field of humanities in general."

"Yes, but what courses in particular?"

"American history and English."

Ellman registered this in silence.

"I know it's an imposition," said Mr. Berger. "And I wouldn't expect you to do it for nothing. If you could see your way clear to give it a try, I'm sure we could work out some sort of an agreement."

"I wouldn't dream of doing it for money," said Ellman. When Mr. Berger began to protest, Ellman countered with, "What about the boy? What does he think?"

"He's willing to try anything. In fact, he's kind of enthusiastic about it because he knows he needs help. He's tried studying by himself but he says these aren't the kind of subjects he can really get a hold on. 'You never know when you know enough.' That's what he told me."

"When can he come up?" Ellman asked.

"We figured he could start Monday night. After that you could work it out between you. Two or three times a week—as often as you can stand him."

"Excellent," said Ellman. "Monday night then. Consider it settled."

Mr. Berger did not reach conclusions so easily, however, and what with assurances of gratitude and sincere but vague promises of working out a financial arrangement, it was fully fifteen minutes before Ellman got him out of the apartment.

As soon as the door closed behind his guest, a younger Julius Ellman took complete control of Ellman's body and filled it with a strange, vibrant excitement.

"A teacher!" he said. "For thirty years I mourn a dead dream and now suddenly it's handed to me on a platter."

He walked around the living room and gripped the back of the chair Mr. Berger had sat in.

"Item for item I could match what he told me. He never finished high school. I never started it. He wanted to be a designer. I wanted to be a teacher. He ends up in a box factory. I end up in the post office. He married young. I married young."

He glanced quickly at the picture of Ruth over the piano and then shifted his gaze to the bookshelf nearby.

"An educated man," he repeated to himself with a smile. "That's what they call you when you fill your life with books. You give up a hope and it becomes a lifelong daydream that transforms every idea you have into a tool that you feel will never be used. And then one day the most unlikely person in the whole world knocks on your door and gives you an opportunity to use all the tools."

He walked to the table, picked up the book he had been reading before Mr. Berger's visit and set it on the bookshelf.

"Be careful, Ellman," he told himself. "Don't let yourself get too enthusiastic. You have less than three months to work with this boy. Three months is not going to make a genius out of anybody."

He cleared off the table in the living room and laid several pieces of writing paper in the center of it.

"There must be a plan," he said. "You have to make a plan and stick to it."

He went to the open closet in the bedroom. In a few minutes, he was happily buried in a pile of notebooks.

Chapter 3

Listen, my children, and you shall hear
The beep-beep-beep from the stratosphere.
On the fourth of October in fifty-seven
Sputnik went to its place in heaven
And round the world people scanned the skies
And those without telescopes strained their eyes
Trying to view the new sensation,
Cause of our latest investigation.
Some of us wondered why "they" were first.
Some of us prayed and some of us cursed.
Some discoursed on cosmic friction
While others boned up on Science Fiction.
We read a great deal on the "race to the stars,"
There were volunteers for the trip to Mars.
Speeches were made about Education
And who would man the first space station.
Some scientists said we were left in a lurch
Because of a lag in our basic research.
The services of our united nation
Were scored for their lack of cooperation.
It's been said as well, "The chief cause was financial,
While all the rest was circumstantial."
Whatever the cause, when all views have been heard,

"Vanguard" remains an embarrassing word.
And as for the future, *we* may regain face,
Though at present it seems that *they're* setting the pace.
So listen, my children, attentively too,
For our real future state will depend upon you.
For you'll be the objects of our dedication,
The pawns in the game of Reformed Education.
And someday, though you may not think it a boon,
You'll inherit the earth and a trip to the moon.

When his poem "Reflections on Sputnik" was published in the *Postal Workers' Monthly* for December, 1957, all of his fellow mail sorters agreed that Courtney Callahan had really caught the "tempo of the times," and that with his brains he was wasting his time at the post office.

"No," Callahan said, with more bitterness than modesty. "It was just amateur stuff. Amateur."

Callahan was thirty-five then and he had the habits and outlook of a middle-aged bachelor. Few of his co-workers at the post office knew that he had ever been married, let alone that he had three children, all of whom were being brought up by his wife's parents, to whom Callahan sent thirty dollars a week board. For the most part he kept to himself and, until the publication of the poem, was regarded by most of his postal acquaintances as a loner and a bit of a grouch.

The poem—or the "doggerel" as Callahan called it—had been written in the course of a single afternoon following a weekend's reading of the *New York Times, Newsweek, Time, Life*, the *New York Daily News* and the *Postal Workers' Monthly*, all of which except the last-named had had serious comment to make upon the sudden appearance of Sputnik I. His sending the poem to the *Monthly* was only an afterthought. Having written it, he thought he might enjoy seeing it published, and if the *Postal Workers' Monthly* was not exactly a mass-circulation magazine, at least it was read by the kind of people Callahan knew and understood. Also, since it published only material written by postal workers, he had a little edge on the formidable competition in the unrestricted "literary" world.

One of the people who read the poem was Julius Ellman, who worked in the same branch as Callahan. The poem was the occasion for the first nonbusiness conversation the two had ever had, and that conversation had formed the basis of a friendship that had lasted down to the present day. Callahan and Ellman seemed to have a great deal in common. Both had come from strong traditional backgrounds, Callahan the Irish Catholic and Ellman the Jewish; and both had felt somehow cut off from their backgrounds, Ellman because his father had been an atheist and Callahan because he had been divorced.

Ellman was the only one to whom Callahan could talk about books without feeling ridiculous and Callahan was the only one to whom Ellman could express his fascination with "the progress of the human mind" without being ridiculed or condescended to. True, they were each aware at times of their own mediocrity—the sour remnant of what in their youth had been a callow eagerness— and there were times when they had avoided one another's company, each imagining for a time that he would be stronger alone and each realizing after a while that there was nothing in lonely strength but strong loneliness. But now, past the age of dreaming that the future would bring fulfillment, they cared nothing for what the rest of the world thought of them and spoke to each other as though they were two philosophers, in a language that was at times ludicrously at variance with the lives they led and the work they did.

The language came more effortlessly to Ellman than it did to Callahan.

"Sure, *you* can read and quote and discuss abstractions," Callahan told him once. "*You* have the qualifications for it.

Your father was a teacher, your brother a musician and, most of all, you're Jewish."

"What does that have to do with it?" Ellman asked.

"A Jew can do these things with dignity," Callahan explained. "He has a tradition to uphold him. An Irishman can do them only at the risk of being called a crank."

When Ellman reminded him that the Irish had a reputation for being an eloquent, poetic race, Callahan countered with the argument that his father had been a longshoreman who beat his kids up every payday and that his brothers were all either longshoremen themselves or truck drivers.

"But me, I was the smart one," he said. "Too smart for my own good. Or maybe I was just saved from being like them by my bad liver. I can't drink liquor without getting deadly sick. So as well as a bad liver, I have a bad temper."

Sometimes Ellman chaffed Callahan with the suggestion that he was actually lying about his background.

"Whatever you say, you sound Jewish," Ellman said. "Sometimes I think you're even more Jewish than I am."

"Sure I feel the Jewish influence," Callahan explained. "I'm taken for Jewish more often than Irish. If my name wasn't Callahan, nobody'd believe I wasn't from Israel. Hell, I'm a New Yorker living in New York. What am I supposed to sound like?"

Ellman shrugged. "Do your brothers sound Jewish?" he asked.

"My brothers!" Callahan repeated scornfully, going off on a tangent that he did not articulate to Ellman and returning with the observation that "I should have followed the races and played the numbers and ended up sitting in the Automat talking with the other snuffy old men about all the big shots they've known in their time."

Instead of playing the numbers, Callahan had dreamed his dreams, read his books and written his verses, none of which had ever been published except the Sputnik one.

It was when he mentioned the mnemonic idea to Ellman that the series of weekly visits made by Ellman to Callahan's furnished room on Twenty-first Street had begun.

"It'd be like a weekly column," he explained. "We could do it for the Sunday *Times*. Just like somebody makes up a crossword or a Double-Crostic for them, we could do a mnemonics page every week. Maybe just a little poem, a verse that would help people remember something important. The names of the states, the members of Congress, candidates for office, the astronauts' names, anything like that."

The idea appealed to Ellman because it seemed to combine his two greatest interests, the training of the mind and current events. In his discussions with Callahan, Ellman always took a lively interest in current affairs, especially since he had once, as he explained to Callahan, "been involved with the labor movement." All Callahan could gather about the involvement, however, was that shortly before coming to work for the post office, he had worked in a dress factory and was fired for attempting to get it unionized.

"To get them interested, we'd have to start with something big," Callahan said. "We need a whole article that will bring a lot of reader response. Say, a four-line verse so packed with meaning that it will take five thousand words to explain all the information contained in it. All the rhyming words are keys to one thing, the first letters of each word spell something else, the first and last words of each line mean another thing. Things like that."

It was an impossible scheme, and they both recognized it as such. But if such men as themselves, with no families to distract them and no serious work to satisfy them, had no time for impossible schemes, then who did?

It was to work on the "mnemonic poem" that they got together every Thursday night. Ellman usually arrived at about seven-thirty and for an hour and a half they would discuss the idea. Tonight, however, the older man seemed anxious to discuss the new teaching project that had come his way.

"You're going to be a tutor?" Callahan asked.

Ellman told him about Mr. Berger's visit and ended with an apology for not having been able to concentrate his attention at all on the mnemonic while making preparations to help Marsh.

"I understand," Callahan said. "But how about this? Suppose we combine the two projects? I could do some sort of a mnemonic poem about American history or English grammar."

"I had thought of that," Ellman said. "Maybe we could use it later. I was in the secondhand stores today buying up textbooks on American history. I'll bring them over sometime and maybe we can begin working out something then."

"You'll have to make up a code for the dates," Callahan said.

"Dates?" Ellman repeated, as if the word had no meaning at all for him.

"Sure. That's mostly what American history is—dates. 'In fourteen hundred and ninety-two, Columbus sailed the ocean blue.'"

Ellman was still staring blankly at him, so Callahan improvised a paraphrase.

"In eighteen hundred and sixty-five, Abraham Lincoln took his dive."

Ellman's expression changed from one of incomprehension to one of incredulous distaste.

"For God sakes, I'm only kidding," Callahan said. "I know how crude it sounds."

"Crude?" Ellman said. He waved his right arm in a gesture that suggested a teacher erasing a blackboard. "It's not the crudity of rhymes and images I mind, but the crudity of dates themselves."

"Dates are raw facts. Raw facts are what a kid has to memorize."

"History is not something to be memorized," Ellman said firmly. "History is something to be experienced and understood."

"That's a fine philosophic point," Callahan said. "But who asked you to teach the kid philosophy?"

Ellman got up from the chair he had been sitting in and, as there was no room for pacing in Callahan's small furnished room, he sat down again immediately and launched into a series of cramped generalizations about American history and the beauties of the English language.

Because he knew it would bring Ellman down to earth again, even if it did irritate him, Callahan suggested that he could do a mnemonic on the parts of speech.

"Parts of speech!" Ellman exploded in disgust.

"Ellman, this boy has to pass a school examination. All his parents want you to do is cram him with some solid information."

"Solid information clings to a generalization like dirt clings to a gardener's hands. Let him concentrate on understanding and the facts will marshal themselves. Marshal themselves!"

Ellman beamed as though he had made an unwitting joke.

"Marshall is the boy's name," he explained.

Callahan did not attempt a smile.

"There will be time for the mnemonics of solid fact," Ellman said. "But that will come later. First there is an attitude that must be formed. A curiosity that must be awakened."

"How are you going to do that?" Callahan asked.

"I don't know," Ellman said. "I've been thinking of ways, but . . . I just don't know yet."

"How can you not know?" Callahan demanded. "You say the kid is coming to you on Monday. All right, he walks into your house on Monday night, sits down and says, 'Here I am. Teach me American history and English.' What's the first thing you do?"

Ellman did not know. And it maddened Callahan that he could not make Ellman see how damning his not knowing was. Ellman's confidence was based on nothing. He simply had an enormous faith in a source of inspiration about which Callahan could only be skeptical.

As was their custom on nights when they worked on the mnemonic, they proceeded from Callahan's room to the Automat on Twenty-third Street. By the time they sat down with their trays of coffee and cake before them, Callahan was striking as urgent a note as he could.

"Ellman, I've never seen you like this," he said. "It's as though you had no sense at all. Look, you're a man who's carried responsibility all his life. And here you get yourself involved in a crazy scheme that can affect a kid's whole career."

"Why is it crazy?" Ellman asked sharply.

"Suppose something goes wrong?" Callahan asked. "Anything at all. You know who'll have to take the whole blame for it? No matter what the reason is, if that kid doesn't pass his test and get admitted to that college, it will be your fault."

"I accept that," Ellman said.

"You accept it without even thinking about it!" Callahan exploded. "Look, don't misunderstand me. I'm not *wishing* hard luck on you, but it bothers me that you don't even seem to *imagine* the idea of failure."

"Why should I?" Ellman said, vaguely aware that he was about to paraphrase one of his inspirational books. "Nothing breeds failure like the thought of failure."

Callahan retreated.

"All right," he said. "Let's assume that you succeed. You even turn this kid into a genius of some kind. What happens then? Let me tell you something. I know kids. So if it's gratitude you're looking for, you can forget it."

"Not gratitude," Ellman said. "Gratification. I want to see this work. Don't you understand that? This is something I've looked for all my life. The chance to enrich another mind. To see it grow and develop under my very eyes. To see it reach its full power while the body is still young enough to make full use of that power. Because of me this boy will have opportunities that you and I never dreamed of. For the sake of that, I'm prepared to take all the risks that you seem so pessimistic about."

When Ellman spoke like that, there were a thousand things Callahan could have said about his vanity and foolishness. And yet, when Ellman spoke like that, Callahan knew that he was speaking to him as he spoke to no one else on earth. For the sake of their friendship he remained silent.

Ellman took his silence as a sign of respect.

Chapter 4

Marshall Berger was nervous as he climbed the one flight to Julius Ellman's apartment on Monday night. His father had sent him off with high hopes but his mother had acted throughout the whole weekend as if Marsh were some sort of sacrificial lamb. Her last words to him as he left the house for his first interview with his new tutor were "Don't pay any attention to what he says."

For himself, Marsh felt that, in a sense, he *was* making a kind of sacrifice—offering his youthful freshness to be smothered under an old stuffiness, all for the sake of money and a career. He wouldn't mind spending a few months under Ellman's tutelage so long as Ellman was able to teach him a trick or two, or give him a key that would unlock all the mysteries of English grammar and American history.

He was rehearsing a few words of introduction—"I'm Marshall Berger"—when he knocked on the old man's door.

Ellman opened the door and smiled as though he and Marsh had been lifelong companions.

"Marshall," he said warmly. "Come in."

Ellman had every light in his apartment turned on, but as soon as Marsh heard the door close behind him he was filled with a sense of gloom and oppression. The apartment he stood in was completely different from the one he had just left, and the contrast was heightened by the fact that the floor plans of Ellman's and his parents' apartments were exactly the same. Ellman had a big round table with four wooden chairs around it, smack dab in the middle of the living room. Over in the corner, where Mrs. Berger had the color television with the plastic flowers in a vase on top of it, Ellman had a heavy-looking old upright piano on top of which rested a dusty violin case. There was no couch in the room but there were two overstuffed chairs, one by the window and another in a corner opposite the piano. Behind one of the chairs stood a lamp the like of which Marsh had never seen before. It had a long neck at the top, and was positioned so that the shade would hang immediately above the head of anyone sitting in the chair. The side of the room on which Mrs. Berger had her couch and coffee table were, in Ellman's apartment, occupied by bookshelves. Against the opposite wall, where Mrs. Berger kept what she called her "knickknack rack," Ellman had only a knobby end table, much higher than any of the end tables Marsh's mother had. On the bottom shelf of this table rested a phonograph which looked as if it had been manufactured in the year One. The top of the table was occupied by a woebegone ten-inch television set.

"I don't use it much anymore," Ellman said, seeing Marsh's eyes come to rest on the television. "But it still works."

Even sounds were different in Ellman's apartment. Marsh was used to the vibrant sound of his radio, the strong drone of the television set, the click of heels on the vinyl floor coverings. Even the crackle of a plastic slipcover or the rustle of a plastic drape would have been welcome to him. But in Ellman's apartment it was all thick chairs, heavy drapes and a faded rug. The room not only looked oppressive, it positively sounded stuffy.

Ellman offered him one of the hard chairs at the table in the center of the living room.

"Sit down," the old man said.

Ellman, too, seemed different to Marsh. It took him some time to figure out that the reason Ellman looked older and frailer than he had ever seemed before was that this was the first time Marsh had ever seen him in his shirtsleeves.

For his own part, Ellman felt he was bustling about with the agility of a schoolboy, an agility which expressed itself in the vigor with which he had swung the door open for the boy and the grace with which he now pulled out a chair for him.

Marsh set his books on the table.

"These are the texts we use at school," he said.

"I see," answered Ellman. He was disappointed at the bald crudity with which Marsh had taken the lead in getting down to business, but he decided not to interpret it as an offense. Put it down as an expression of the boy's eagerness, he told himself. See it as the measure of his need.

Ellman took the books from in front of Marsh and glanced briefly at the titles.

"We won't be needing these for a while yet," he said, putting them down on top of the piano.

Marsh looked puzzled but he said nothing.

"Would you like a drink of water?" Ellman asked. "Maybe coffee or tea?"

Marsh said no.

"Let me bring in the water anyway," Ellman said. "I was just rinsing out the pitcher when you knocked."

Ellman disappeared into the kitchen and returned after a moment with a small tray containing a pitcher of water and two glasses.

"I'll have the water later," Ellman said. "Right now it's coffee I want."

He disappeared into the kitchen again. Marsh glanced at his watch and wondered if Ellman was planning an English lesson or a social evening.

Ellman returned with a cup of coffee, a saucer and a spoon. He set them on the table, sat down opposite Marsh and, for a long time, gave his full attention to the business of stirring his coffee.

"Now then," he said when the coffee had finally been stirred to taste. "It's about time we started, isn't it?"

Marsh grinned involuntarily and shrugged.

"The less time we waste, the less time we lose," Ellman said. "So suppose you begin by telling me the story of America."

For a moment the words did not seem to make sense.

"The what?" asked Marsh.

"American history is only the story of America," said Ellman. "I want you to tell me that story."

Marsh drew less of a blank this time, but he still felt a little off balance.

"I don't know where to begin," he said.

"Once upon a time," said Ellman, leaning back in his chair, "there was a man named Columbus."

Slowly, Marsh began. There was a man named Columbus and then, somehow, there was a settlement at Jamestown. Oh, yes, there was Henry Hudson too, and Peter Minuit buying Manhattan Island for twenty-four dollars.

"His own men put him off the ship in a boat," Marsh said.

"Whose?"

"Henry Hudson. The sailors set him adrift in Hudson Bay. Him and his son."

No detail was too small for Ellman. When Marsh casually mentioned something about Pocahontas, Ellman insisted that he tell the whole story about her and Captain John Smith.

After he had elicited from Marsh all the names and interesting anecdotes he could about the early explorers, Ellman shifted the recitation to the colonial period. He did everything he could to throw Marsh's mind wide open on the subject, even down to letting him describe the plots of historical movies he had seen.

Ellman was in the kitchen pouring himself a cup of coffee while Marsh rattled on about Priscilla Mullens and "Speak for yourself, John." He had begun the story under the vague impression that speak-for-yourself John was Captain John Smith, but interrupted himself to announce, "No it wasn't. It was Captain Miles Standish."

Ellman returned from the kitchen smiling.

Marsh frowned. "But then who was speak-for-yourself *John?*"

"I believe his name was John Alden," Ellman said slowly.

Ellman never allowed Marsh's recital to become a discussion between the two of them. He merely supplied a word here or a hint there in order to keep the boy's flow going, to prevent him from losing himself in the search for some irrelevant detail. His only reference was a secondhand history text he had bought over the weekend.

Marsh's voice quickly became thick with so much talking but he was pleased to realize, as he helped himself to his first glass of the ice water Ellman had set out on the table for him, that the sense of stuffiness which had overcome him when he first entered the apartment had left him completely His mind was alive and glowing and it was still glowing an hour later while, with Ellman gone to the kitchen again to refill the water pitcher, he struggled to remember just what George Washington was doing in Valley Forge and why it was so necessary for him to cross the Delaware that night.

Marsh was explaining the results of the War of 1812 when Ellman interrupted him to suggest that they bring this first lesson to a close. It was then ten o'clock.

"Ten o'clock!" Marsh repeated incredulously. "You mean I've been here for two and a half hours?"

Ellman smiled and nodded.

"I talked for two and a half hours! And we barely got to Jackson."

"The wonder is that we got as far as we did," said the tutor.

"Compressing three hundred and twenty years into two and a half hours is no small feat."

"Three hundred and twenty years!" said Marsh.

"I'm afraid I've turned you into an echo," said Ellman, smiling. "At any rate, I think you'd better go downstairs before your parents come up looking for you."

Marsh gathered his books and prepared to leave.

"One more thing," said Ellman. "It occurs to me that since we never looked at your textbook, you may be wondering just what it was that you learned tonight. For one thing, you may have learned that you know a great deal more than you thought you did."

"That's true," said Marsh. "I also know there's a heck of a lot I don't know."

"About those, I think—er, I should say, I hope—that you're beginning to develop some curiosity."

Marsh grinned and nodded his head.

"Good!" Ellman said. "That's important. Now before I forget, when do you come back next? Is Wednesday all right?"

His mother and father were both watching a spy movie when Marsh came downstairs.

"How did it go?" his father asked. He looked at Marsh when he asked the question, but before Marsh could answer, Mr. Berger's eyes were back on the television set.

"Okay," Marsh said.

He passed through the living room and into the adjoining bedroom, which was his own. Later in the evening, when the eleven o'clock news was over, his father would pass through Marsh's room to the far bedroom. Still later, when the midnight movie was over, Mrs. Berger would also pass through, turning off lights behind her and bumping into Marsh's bed in the dark.

His room was flooded with the sound of the secret-agent movie. Marsh started to set his books in the closet but, on a last-minute impulse, he took the history text and tossed it onto the bed.

"You want something to eat?" his mother called from the next room.

"No, thanks."

Marsh stretched out on the bed and turned on the lamp on his night table.

"A piece of cake maybe? I bought a nice coffee ring."

"Nothing, thanks."

"It's a shame to waste it."

Marsh let the movie do its work. His mother lapsed into silence.

He opened the history book to the first page and began to read the text. He read it not as an assignment, but much in the manner in which he would have read a novel. Marsh was a slow reader, and the forty-three pages he read that night were something of a milestone to him. It was more than he had ever read at one sitting before.

45

Chapter 5

When Marsh picked her up that Thursday to go to the play, Donna was wearing a miniskirt and a fall.

The miniskirt showed most of her legs, which were slim enough to have shape and yet fleshy enough to have substance.

"I've said it before and I'll say it again," Marsh said as they set out on their way to the subway. "With legs like that, you *gotta* be Puerto Rican."

Donna was not pleased with the compliment. "If you like Puerto Ricans so much," she said, "why don't you get yourself one of them to fool around with?"

The fall was a new acquisition. The last time Marsh saw Donna, she had been wearing her hair in little points that met at the cleft of her chin. That hair style was an imitation of Doris Day that Marsh had only just broken himself of the habit of kidding her about. To him it had looked horribly uncomfortable. He could imagine the points sticking in her mouth or at least rubbing against her face and he kept asking her, in all seriousness, if they did not bother her. His concern, however, seemed only to exasperate Donna. When he realized he had found a new way to tease her, Marsh was relentless with his questions.

"How can you eat with these things hanging in front of your mouth? Suppose you had corn on the cob?"

"Why do you let it hang over your face if you're going to keep pushing it back that way anyway?"

"Somebody told me that wearing your hair like that can give you acne. No kidding, the stuff they put in the hair-set collects on your face and gives you a rash."

Donna raged at the cracks, but Marsh did not let up on them until Donna brought up the subject during one of their moments of presex seriousness. She did not make it conditional, but she did not have to. There was a sense between them that anything said at times like that was extra-tender serious and had to be respected. Once or twice Marsh forgot and let fly with a crack but Donna raged no more. She simply stared at him with a reproachful "remember our pact" look, and he repented. Only now, when the habit was completely broken, did Donna change her hair style once more.

"Your hair looks nice like that," Marsh said. "That thing hanging down your back, it does something for you."

"I'm glad you like it," Donna said. "When I'm finished with it, I'll give it to you."

The sign in the lobby described *Adamant Eve* as a "boffo comedy about conformity" and eulogized the star, Alan Horgan, for his "audience-warming" performance as the father whose daughter has elected to "drop out" of society.

During intermission, Marsh overheard a couple of fey types discussing the play in the men's room.

"The play is crummy, of course," one said, "but Horgan is magnificent. He's the whole show."

Marsh repeated the remark to Donna as they went home that night.

"I can't understand people like that," he explained. "It's as if they enjoyed not liking things."

"Personally, I thought it was terrific," Donna said. "That time when she told her father she dropped out and her father said, 'Well, drop back *in* again sometime.' I thought I'd die."

"Then in the end it turns out they were really married all the time—"

"And the leader tells them they have to leave the group. I thought I'd die."

He walked Donna home from the subway, but did not go upstairs. For a long while they stood in the vestibule with their arms around each other.

"Too bad you didn't get the tickets for a Friday," Donna said. "My folks might not have been home."

"Tomorrow's Friday," Marsh said suggestively.

"Which reminds me," Donna said, breaking away from his embrace. "What time are you picking me up for Angie's party?"

"About ten-thirty," Marsh said.

"Why so late?"

"I have another lesson with the tutor tomorrow," Marsh said. "We decided to make it three nights a week instead of two."

They went from the vestibule into the hallway. Donna sat on the steps and asked him how the lessons were going.

"Okay, I guess," Marsh said. "I told you the first session was just great but, after that, when I tried to pick up again where I left off, I just couldn't get warmed up again. Man, the whole thing just dragged and dragged."

"Is that all you do is just talk?" Donna asked.

"So far it is," Marsh said. "Four sessions and I'm just getting through the Second World War. I think we're going to start on English soon. He asked me to give him one of my school compositions. He said he wanted to keep it awhile."

Marsh sat next to Donna on the steps, but she got up again.

"If you're not coming around until ten-thirty," she said, "I may as well go to work tomorrow after all. It's only from four to eight o'clock. I'll still have time to get ready for the party."

"You weren't going to go to work tomorrow?" Marsh said, rising and taking her in his arms again.

"I was going to wait until after school and then call in sick." Marsh's hands were exploring their favorite regions. "Not in the hallway," Donna said, taking hold of his wrists. "Somebody might come along."

"How about under the stairs?" Marsh asked. "It's dark there. Nobody'd see us."

"Okay," Donna said. "But just for a few minutes. All right?"

"All right," Marsh said. "Just a few minutes."

They went under the staircase.

On Monday Marsh had a great deal of homework to do. He had finished everything but the math when it came time to go upstairs. For a moment he considered asking the tutor for the night off, but Mr. Ellman might think he was not taking things seriously if he started cutting now. After all, Ellman was only working for his benefit.

The last session had ended just as the Japanese surrendered after the dropping of the first atomic bomb. Marsh expected that tonight he would bring the story down to the present day in less than an hour, which would leave him time to find out what the old man was planning next. Whatever it was, it would be good to have the unending epic behind him. After only six sessions, Marsh dreaded to hear Ellman speak the words "everything you can remember."

Even though they were never used, Marsh continued to bring his books to every session. Their presence helped him concentrate.

He had just set them down on the table when Ellman asked him what he had done over the weekend. It was the first time he had ever shown any interest in Marsh's private life.

"Parties," Marsh said, sitting down. "Oh, I went to a play on Thursday night. I didn't tell you about that."

"What play?" Ellman asked.

"*Adamant Eve*," Marsh answered. To prevent Ellman from making the same mistake everyone else had made, he stressed the *t* and pronounced the title "Adam Ann *Teeve*." Even in Marsh's own ears his pronunciation sounded affected. His face reflected his discomfort.

"You didn't like it?" Ellman concluded.

"Oh, no, it was great," Marsh said.

Once, while Jacob had been associated with musicals, Julius Ellman had taken some slight interest in the theater, but that interest had long since waned. He had never heard of *Adamant Eve*.

"What was it about?" he asked.

"This guy's daughter joins the hippies and has a baby. It wasn't serious, though, it was funny."

Ellman would not let it go at that. "I was going to discuss that composition you brought me," he said. "But we'll put that aside for a while. Instead we'll make an English lesson of that play you saw. Call it Contemporary Literature. I want you to tell me as much as you can remember of the whole play, starting as the curtain goes up on Act One."

Marsh resisted at first, unwilling to fool himself into believing that a rehash of *Adamant Eve*, even if you called it Contemporary Literature, could help him answer the English questions on the Scholastic Achievement Test. But Ellman held firm and soon Marsh was launched into his narrative. He suppressed some of the details and, as with the history narration, he got a few incidents out of sequence, but in spite of Ellman's thirst for "Details, more details," Marsh brought the curtain down on the play in less than an hour.

"Very good," Ellman said. "Now tell me. What did you *think* of the play?"

Marsh was drugged with boredom and fatigue.

"What's to think?" he said. "It was funny. I enjoyed it."

Ellman was not satisfied with that, of course. He asked Marsh if he thought the hippies were fairly represented in the piece.

"It was a play," Marsh insisted. "The whole idea behind it was just to give you a few laughs."

"But doesn't it seem to you somewhat artificial—phony, if you like? You tell me it turns out they were married all the time. Didn't that seem a bit contrived to you?"

"It could happen," Marsh said.

He thought again of the math homework that remained to be done when he got downstairs.

"I thought we were going to finish up the history thing tonight," he said.

"All in good time," Ellman said. "But let me ask you one question first: Have you ever considered 'dropping out' yourself?" Ellman pronounced the words "dropping out" in cautious isolation, as one does when using a phrase for the first time.

"I don't see how this is going to help me on the test," Marsh protested.

"It's not important for you to see at this stage," Ellman said. "I can't explain myself every step of the way. Trust me, all this will help you with your schoolwork. With English, with American history and with a lot of other things that you'll be studying later on."

Marsh clearly did not understand. He swiveled around in his chair, hunched his shoulders, crossed his arms and said, "No."

"No?" Ellman repeated. "No, what?"

"I never thought of dropping out."

For a moment Ellman did not say anything. Marsh was fully aware that the old man had misunderstood his first "No."

"I didn't mean I thought you had *decided* on it," Ellman said. "But surely you must have thought about it."

"No," Marsh answered.

Ellman had been sitting at the table. He now got up to pour himself another one of his everlasting cups of coffee.

"Your father tells me you want to become an engineer," he called from the kitchen.

"An electronics engineer," Marsh said. "At least, that's what I used to want. I may change and go in for computer programming. That's where the big money is now. In computers."

"Then of course you wouldn't be thinking of dropping out," Ellman said.

"I don't want to talk abut dropping out or dropping in," Marsh said gruffly. "Talk about phoniness; if you ask me, that's where the real phoniness is. What's wrong with wanting to get a good job at a good salary so you can get the best out of life?"

Ellman returned to the living room.

"Who said there was anything wrong with it?" he asked. "I was just inquiring about your plans, your future."

Ellman told Marsh about his nephews, Norman and Nathan, and about their jobs. He made it all sound very comfortable and pleasant.

"In fact," he summed up, "I'd say that what my nephews have is very much like what you plan for yourself. The sort of life they lead seems to be very much what you want."

"It's what everybody wants," Marsh asserted.

Ellman smiled. "Maybe I've painted too rosy a picture," he said. "To my nephews sometimes it seems to be nothing but a lot of bills and headaches."

Marsh took the English text off the table and began thumbing through it.

"If I'd really been smart," he said, "I would have gone to a vocational high school. Then I'd really learn something I could use. I mean, when you come down to it, isn't it really a waste of time to study English?"

Ellman was pained. "If you mean because you've been speaking it all your life," he said, "then I don't agree with you.

But there is a sense in which I do agree. I was reading in a magazine last week about some people who are studying facial expressions and hand movements because they've just discovered what sensible people have known all along—that we communicate with our bodies as well as with our words. And they're drawing diagrams of our facial expressions and inventing symbols for our body movements. Now all this is very fine and interesting for the present. But I'm afraid the day will come when they'll put all this together into a *grammar* of body movement and you'll have dried-up teachers like me telling you that, in certain circumstances, a raised eyebrow is grammatically incorrect. It's that kind of English teaching I don't hold with."

"Maybe there'd be some point in learning Spanish," Marsh said. "But I've had two years of it now and I still can't speak it."

"Do you want to speak Spanish?"

"No!" Marsh answered. "I mean, it'd be nice and all that if I could, but it's not important. And if I didn't have to study Spanish, I could take the same time I waste on that and use it to study the things that really count."

"And the things that really count are the things that will help you to get this dream job of yours. Is that right?"

"Right."

"But one of the requirements for this dream job is that it must have an early retirement plan?"

"Twenty years at most."

"Which means that you'll still be comparatively young when you retire. Now tell me, what will you do with all this time you'll have on your hands then?"

Marsh grinned in a way that he thought knowing and Ellman thought ugly.

"I'll find things to do," Marsh said. "There's a lot more to life than books."

Ellman's eyes darted to the bookshelf. As Marsh's eyes followed them there, he remembered a little of what the old man had said about communicating with more than words.

"I think we were about at the end of the Second World War when we concluded last time," the tutor said abruptly. "Why don't we pick it up there now."

After Marsh had left, Ellman took his newspaper and consulted the ABC theater listings. The play was not really the sort of thing he would have attended on his own, of course, but he felt it might help him to understand Marsh a bit better if he went to see the play that Marsh had enjoyed so much.

Chapter 6

Ernest had been warned by his father that he was not to return that afternoon without the tickets. For a week now, Ernest had been finding one excuse after another to put the distasteful task off. His mother had even offered to go down and get the tickets for him, but his father forbade it.

"He'll get the tickets himself," he insisted. "I'm sick of this nonsense. He can't do this and he can't do that. If it's reached a point where he can't even walk up to a window and buy a couple of tickets, then I say it's time we put a stop to it."

To Ernest, his instructions were quite explicit. "I want you to get those tickets and I want them here when I come home tonight. Two in the orchestra for Friday night. On the aisle."

Ernest was not able to concentrate on his schoolwork at all that morning. At lunchtime he bought the usual ham sandwich and milk but found, after one bite, that he was unable to eat.

Suppose they had no tickets left for Friday night. If Ernest came back empty-handed his father would never believe he had even gone to the theater. Or suppose they had tickets for Friday but not in the orchestra? Suppose they had orchestra seats but not on the aisle. Suppose he bought Friday-night orchestra seats but they were way over on the side? His father would holler all over the place that they probably had good seats all the time but that they did not give them to Ernest because he hadn't the guts to speak up for himself. He might even make Ernest take the tickets back for a refund or exchange.

His father had given him twenty-five dollars, assuring him that that would be more than enough. But suppose his father was wrong? Friday was the beginning of the weekend. Suppose they had special high prices for weekends?

Ernest took out his wallet, checked his father's money and then looked in a separate compartment where he kept his own cash. He had nine dollars of his own as a margin for safety, but even as he put the wallet back in his pocket he could hear his father roaring at him. "I gave you twenty-five dollars. If I'd known it was more than that, I wouldn't have wanted the damned tickets at all. Take them down and get your money back."

His heart jumped a bit when he finally arrived on the block where the theater was. ADAMANT EVE, the marquee proclaimed. SMASH COMEDY.

He stopped outside to study the posters and photographs for a while. He found the picture of Alan Horgan, with its expression of battered, paternal bewilderment, particularly repulsive. After studying the picture for a moment, he began to walk down the block. After two full turns around the block he was ready to enter the theater.

There were five people on the line in front of the box office in the lobby. Ernest hoped that the line would move quickly so that there would be no one behind him when he got to the window. He strained his ears to hear what the man at the head of the line was saying to the ticket seller.

"No, I need all ten together. It's for an organization. The twentieth will be fine."

The twentieth was three weeks away. Now if they had ten seats together on the twentieth, would that increase or decrease the possibility of their having two aisle seats available for Friday night? Before Ernest had time to consider this problem too deeply, a tall, elderly man entered the lobby and took his place in line behind Ernest.

Ernest had an impulse to leave the theater and wait outside until there was no one waiting in line, but he was afraid that such a time would never come. So he stood his ground while the first man paid for and collected his ten tickets. Then there were only four people in front of him.

The ten-ticket man did not leave the theater immediately. He walked to the opposite end of the lobby and stood there for a moment, consulting his tickets and checking them against a large seating diagram that Ernest had not noticed before.

Ernest decided on one more stalling maneuver. He would walk to the seating diagram and study it for a while. Then he would return to the box office and take his place *behind* the old man who had just come in.

He had no sooner set his eyes on the seating diagram than Ernest found himself in another quandary. The theater had no center aisle. It had a center section and two side aisles. Did his father ask for an aisle seat, then, because he thought it would be in the center where he would have a better view, or did he want an aisle seat because, like Ernest, he did not like to have people hemming him in on both sides?

Ernest frowned, scratched his head and looked over toward the box office as though he could find an answer there.

The old man who had been behind him had also left his place in line and was now approaching the seating diagram.

Ernest turned away. He had gotten all he could from the diagram but if he went back to the line now, the old man would come shortly after, take the position behind Ernest once more, and everything would be as it had been before. Scarcely conscious of what he was doing, Ernest began rummaging violently through his pockets.

The old man nodded and smiled at Ernest as he reached the seating diagram. Ernest's frown deepened and he began pulling things out of his pockets. His wallet, his handkerchief, his key ring, a slip of white paper with the title, author and publisher of a book he had to buy for school written on it.

"Have you lost something?" the old man asked.

Ernest stared hard at the piece of paper, as though it were the object he had been seeking. Then he shook his head dramatically, left the theater and took another turn around the block.

When he returned to the lobby, all was as it had been before, except that there were now only three people on the line. The old man gave him a glance of recognition as Ernest entered, but he quickly turned around again and did not offer any conversation. Ernest took the place behind him, determined that he would stay put this time and see it through to the end.

The old man bought a ticket for the Wednesday matinee.

"Just one," he said. "Anyplace in the balcony will do."

Ernest's luck held. There was no one behind him when at last he stood in front of the box office window.

"Yes?" the ticket seller said. "What do you want?"

Ernest hesitated for a moment, hoping the old man would move away. Instead he stood there carefully examining his ticket and making an elaborate show of buttoning up his overcoat before venturing out into the street.

"Well?" said the ticket seller.

The sentence was quite clear in Ernest's mind: *Two seats in the middle for Friday night.*

"T-t-two," he said.

"Two what?" the ticket seller said.

Out of the corner of his eye Ernest noticed a definite stiffening of the old man's spine as he listened to Ernest. Now, without any pretense of buttoning his coat or fussing with his ticket, he stood perfectly still. He, like the ticket seller, was waiting for Ernest's next word.

"F-F-Friday," Ernest said.

"Two for Friday," the ticket seller summarized. "Okay, where do you want them? In the orchestra or upstairs?"

With a sudden, lurching movement, the old man walked out of Ernest's range of vision. A moment later, Ernest heard one of the lobby doors open and he knew he was alone with the ticket seller.

The business of buying the tickets was still an agony, but Ernest got through it by dispensing with the niceties. Having communicated the fact that he wanted the seats to be in the center section, he gave up the idea of insisting that they be in the center of the center, and not too far to the right, left, front or back.

The seats were eleven dollars apiece, so his father had not been so far off about the price. Ernest checked the seating diagram. The location seemed awfully far back to him, but a sign over the diagram announced reassuringly that every seat in the theater had a clear and unobstructed view of the stage.

Anyway, he had the tickets. The battle was won. And if his father didn't like the location, he could take the tickets back himself.

It was brisk and cool outside. Ellman jammed his hands into his pockets as soon as the theater door closed behind him. He turned and began walking east.

When he reached Third Avenue he turned south. A few blocks on he came to a small store that had the appearance of an old-fashioned ice cream parlor, although the sign identified it as a coffee shop. He went inside and sat at the counter, noting with satisfaction that it was a good, solid marble counter and not one of those gleaming formica counter tops that glared at one everywhere these days.

There were two people behind the counter. From the way they spoke to one another, Ellman judged them to be husband and wife. Again he was satisfied. The business was a family business and that meant that perhaps there would be some show of pride or at least interest in the service provided there.

The man stood at the back of the counter with a stack of papers in front of him. He stared at each paper, made an entry in a book and then impaled the paper on a spike, a device Ellman had not seen used in years.

The woman approached Ellman.

"What'll it be?" she asked.

"Coffee," Ellman said. "Just coffee."

He was pleased with his articulation of the words. No hesitation, no contractions in the throat, no paralysis of the jaw. In short, no stutter. Just the effortless expression of his thought.

"Coffee," he said again. "Just coffee."

"All right," the woman said, smiling in a way that showed she was more amused than offended at his apparent impatience.

Ellman had not realized that he was speaking aloud the second time.

"I'm sorry," he said quickly. "I wasn't meaning to rush you."

There! Even when he was upset he could speak clearly, with no trace of the stutter that had plagued him for so many years in his youth.

"Where did it go?" he asked himself. "How did I get over it?"

The woman placed the coffee, milk and sugar in front of him.

"Anything else?" she asked.

"No, thank you," he answered. "This will be fine."

It was difficult for Ellman to remember now the days in his early childhood when there was no trace of a speech impediment of any kind. During his boyhood years, it sometimes seemed to him that he had always had difficulty with his speech and that he probably always would have difficulty with it. In the second grade he had a teacher named Miss Morris, who firmly believed that the best way to cure his stutter was to rap him across the knuckles every time he spoke. And yet he could remember that when his mother took him to school for the first time, she had chided him for babbling and warned him that he would soon be in trouble if he tried talking that much in school.

So it was sometime in between the first and second grades that Ellman had begun to stutter.

Of course! There was no mystery about it. Ellman recalled now that he had trod this ground many times before. His stutter must have developed shortly after his brother Jacob had been born. Strange, the way he kept remembering that fact and then dismissing it.

"It was not significant," Ellman said aloud.

It was not that Ellman thought himself to be above feeling jealous of the new baby. No, he rejected Jacob's birth as a cause of his stutter mainly because it did not fit in with the rest of the facts.

In the long years of Julius Ellman's torture, his brother Jacob was the only person to whom he could speak without stuttering. Even his parents' presence caused him to stammer uncontrollably. Later, of course, there had been Ruth, but even in his first few meetings with her the stutter had been an obstacle.

Never with Jacob.

Strangely, they had never discussed the stutter. Jacob was aware of it, of course. Many times they had been together in their room when their mother came in to ask a casual question and while Julius struggled to squeeze out an answer, Jacob would help him by forming the word with his lips, not venturing to answer aloud any question that Julius took as being directed at him and yet wanting to help Julius in his fight to form the right word.

Others were always suggesting cures. Even though Julius had difficulty in getting off even a simple one-word answer, his father thought that tongue twisters would be a sound device for untwisting his eldest son's tongue. Night after night he and Julius would sit in the kitchen together, the father rattling on about Peter Piper picking his peck of pickled peppers and the son going into a cataleptic fit before the first *P*.

The heartbreaking thing was that when he was alone the twisters gave him no trouble at all. His boxes of biscuits never got mixed with his biscuit mixers and each speech trotted trippingly off his tongue. Once, after drilling for the whole of a Sunday afternoon, Julius planned to surprise his father at dinnertime by rattling off a whole series of twisters, one after another. He rehearsed the scene several times. Just as dinner was ready, he would go into the bathroom to wash his hands so that the others would be seated at the table by the time he entered the kitchen. He would take his place at the table then and, before there was even a chance to develop any nervousness, he would begin, starting with the twister about the formidable Peter Piper.

Everything went according to plan until he sat down and opened his mouth.

His father had looked at him and Julius had known the scheme was not going to work.

His mouth was open. It was plain that he was about to speak. His father leaned forward to join him in the struggle. Even Jacob, who was only five at the time, knew that when Julius was trying to speak it was a time for everyone else to be silent and listen.

Julius had braced himself as he felt the first contraction in his throat. He was determined not to let the first *P* pass his lips until he was certain that he could shape it firmly into a flaring "Peter Piper."

He concentrated on forming the word. It was coming. He was g-g-getting it. And even in the act of getting it, he was stuttering. Stuttering!

He took a deep breath and swallowed as hard as he could.

"P-p-p-" he said.

No! Call it a false start. He swallowed again.

His father's lined face revealed how clearly he was sharing his son's anguish.

It was apparent that Julius had already lost all chance of giving his father the surprise he had planned. Tears began to well up in his eyes. He gripped the edge of the table and braced himself for another attempt.

"P-p-p-"

Even if he said it now, he would still have failed. Erase that attempt and start again. He had to get it on a first try or not at all.

"P-p-p-"

His father gestured at the dinner table before them.

"Potatoes?" he suggested softly.

Julius had fled back into the bathroom.

Even now, finishing his coffee in the ice cream parlor–coffeehouse, Ellman could not find it in his heart to laugh at that long forgotten bread-and-butter tragedy.

"Where can I get a downtown bus?" he called to the woman behind the counter.

"One block over, one block down," the woman said.

The blocks in this part of town had a way of seeming endlessly long. Ellman knew he had already walked farther for one day than he should have.

"Let me have another cup of coffee," he said. "Can I take it in one of those booths?"

He felt much more comfortable sitting in a booth than he had at the counter. True, there was not quite enough room for him to stretch his legs out as far as he would have liked, but he was still better off settled on the soft upholstery than he had been perched on a stool.

He remembered the last job he had had before he started with the post office. The Steamer Trunk Dress Company. He had not been one of the organizers of the strike, but he had been one of the token handful that the police arrested for illegal picketing. He could still remember the jail, and see the courtroom as it had looked that night, still recall how jubilant his companions had been, as if to be arrested were the greatest privilege they could enjoy.

The moment he was arrested, Ellman had begun to suffer terrible pains of anguish. The hours they spent in jail before appearing in night court were sheer agony for him. The others from Steamer Trunk, intoxicated with their own excitement, all more or less assumed that he too must be delighted with the way things had turned out. After all, he had even less to lose than any of the others among them. He had no family to care for, no one depending on him. He was free, if he so chose, to give himself over completely to the cause of the workers.

"You should be glad," Freddy Kitch told him. "You're one of the chosen few. That's a great distinction."

Ellman was glad to be among the chosen, but he was terrified thinking what might happen when he had to stand up alone in court. The others, he knew, would jeer at the judge, wave at those of their fellow workers who appeared in court and harangue any representative of Steamer Trunk's management who might show up. But Ellman himself would tremble and shake, taking half an hour just to speak his name and address to the court.

Freddy Kitch had started singing a song of the worker movement and the others had joined him. Ellman, without forming the words, began to hum along with the others, enjoying the sound of his voice blending with the others' and the occasional harmonic tickle in his ear when, by some accident, they were all on pitch. Soon he attempted to sing the words and, to his delight, found that he had no difficulty with them. By the time the guard came to quiet them down and bring them into the courtroom, Ellman was full of confidence and high spirits, determined to do nothing that would let his comrades down.

When he stood up in court, though, he was alone again. He stuttered over his name, as he had expected to, and there was a painful silence in the court while he gave his address and struggled to explain that he "b-b-boarded w-w-with a c-c-c-cousin" of his mother's. He was almost overcome with a sense of his own failure when he remembered the companions standing behind him and the confidence their singing had inspired him with. Expecting to be carried along miraculously by the sheer force and importance of his message, Ellman then launched himself into what was to have been a speech about the labor movement. It had aborted itself into a series of nervous rasps about the "s-s-solidarity of the w-w-w-working c-c-cl-classes."

"Asinine!" Ellman said aloud.

"What was that?" the woman behind the counter asked.

"Nothing," Ellman answered. "One block over and one block down is the bus stop, right?"

There was a mirror at the counter behind the cash register. Ellman looked into it and remembered the years of his adolescence, when he had stood in front of the mirror for hours talking to himself, studying the way his lips moved and hypnotizing himself into believing that the next person he spoke to would hear a Julius Ellman whom he had never even suspected existed. The daydream never came true, but nothing could stop him from engaging in it.

Now, looking at himself in the coffeeshop mirror, Ellman saw himself as he had been in his youth—the locked-in personality staring at itself in the mirror and trying to find a way out of its own prison—and he saw himself as he was now, understanding that only time could take care of the stutter, knowing that all his diction exercises and mirror contemplations were just wastes of energy. Wasn't the truth simply that there came a time when whatever it was inside him that caused the stutter had just decided to let go, because he was too old to stutter and because it simply didn't matter anymore?

How impossible it would have been to explain that to the younger Julius Ellman. *You don't understand*, he would have said. *You just don't know what it's like.*

"No," Ellman said. "I don't understand. The answer is lost in my own experience and I still don't understand it. My younger self would have had no patience with the only kind of advice I could give him now."

The woman had come up to collect Ellman's money. He could tell from the expression on her face that she was aware that he had been talking to himself. As she handed him his change he looked her straight in the eye.

"How's that for a generation gap?" he said aloud.

Chapter 7

"Do they still teach you in school to make an outline before you write a composition?" Ellman asked.

Marsh looked at his composition. It was on the general topic "My Hobby." Mr. Cass had given him a C-plus for it.

"We're supposed to," he admitted. "But I usually don't."

"I see."

Ellman read the composition to himself and then rapidly made some notes on a sheet of paper. Working from these notes, he wrote some more on a second sheet. Then he handed both sheets to Marsh.

"This is an analysis of the composition as it's written," he said. "This other page is a rearrangement of that outline in a more orderly fashion. As I see it, the main statement of the composition is the line about the joy you had when you were finally able to listen to a radio that you had put together with your own hands. You've thrown the whole idea away by setting it down in the middle paragraph. To repeat it at the end —and almost in the very same words—only underlines the weakness of the composition. If you want to make it really effective, you have to turn the whole thing inside out. That's what I've tried to do in that second outline."

Marsh took the outlines Ellman had handed him and compared them.

"Do you see what I mean?" Ellman asked.

"Yes," Marsh answered. "This one is better."

Ellman reached across the table, took the original outline away and tore it up.

"I want you to take that revised outline and rewrite the composition from it," he said.

"Do I have to?" Marsh asked.

"You have the outline drawn up already," Ellman said. "It will be easier than you think."

Marsh did not have his watch on, and there was no clock in Ellman's living room, so he could not judge how long it took him to work his way through the writing of another draft, but it seemed a matter of hours. When he had rounded off the last sentence, he shoved the paper away from him and set the pen down with a gasp of relief.

"Finished?" Ellman asked.

Marsh handed him the composition.

"The outline too," said the tutor.

While Ellman studied the new version, Marsh went to the kitchen for a glass of water.

"You've departed from the outline," Ellman said when Marsh came back into the living room. Ellman seized another piece of blank paper and began writing again. "If I analyze the composition the way it's written now," he said, "this is the way the outline would look. Now I want you to compare this outline with the one you were supposed to be working from."

Marsh looked at the papers Ellman handed him and his heart sank. He could see, stretching before him, an endless chain of analyzed compositions, revised outlines and rewritten essays.

"Do you see where it goes off?" Ellman said. "The middle paragraph again."

On the analysis sheet, section 2, subheading B read "Satisfaction." On the original outline Ellman had given him to work from, "Satisfaction" was listed as section 5, subheading A.

"It's not the same thing," Marsh said. He explained to Ellman that in the middle paragraph he had merely meant that one part of the operation had given him satisfaction, but the satisfaction at the end applied to the project as a whole. Ellman, however, preferred to have no mention of satisfaction at all until the end. On the strength of that, he asked Marsh to try writing the composition just one more time.

"Can't we just scratch out that part in the middle?" Marsh asked.

"No," Ellman answered. "I want you to have practice in working on the thing as a whole."

With a little prodding, Ellman agreed to let Marsh dictate the revision from outline, while Ellman himself made notes and corrections on the draft Marsh had written earlier.

"I know this must be a terrible bore for you," Ellman said. "And you must be sick to death of hearing about that blasted radio you made. But believe me, all this will be of inestimable value for you."

As tactfully as he could, Marsh tried to explain to Ellman that his real problem with English came with sentence analysis and vocabulary, but Ellman did not regard these as serious matters.

"Vocabulary is mainly a matter of experience," he said. "As for sentence structure, that's largely a matter of logic. Learn to think clearly and you will have no difficulty in expressing yourself clearly."

Not until Ellman was satisfied that the form of the composition was perfect did they begin working on the grammatical errors. When at last they compared the final version with the original composition, Marsh had to admit that, structurally and grammatically, it was much improved. Nevertheless, he figured that Mr. Cass would have given it an automatic C anyway, because it was too long. The original assignment had called for something between two and three hundred words. Their final draft ran over four hundred.

Marsh did not mention this to Ellman.

Mrs. Berger was off playing bingo when Marsh came downstairs that night. He found his father sitting gloomily in front of the television set, a can of beer gripped tightly in his hand. Marsh went straight to the kitchen. There was a defrosted layer cake on the table. He cut himself a piece and then took down a glass for milk.

The refrigerator had three milk containers in it, but one of them had only a drop left. Marsh drank this and put a full container on the table next to the glass. The empty container he carried to the garbage can in the corner, where he found three empty beer cans.

"Bring me another beer while you're there," Mr. Berger called.

Marsh grinned and went to the refrigerator.

"How'd it go tonight?" his father asked when Marsh delivered the beer and began to settle himself in the living room.

"Not so good," Marsh said. "We did a lot of work on an old composition of mine, then we talked about a play Mr. Ellman went to see this afternoon. The same one I saw last week."

"What play is that?" Mr. Berger asked.

Marsh winced. "It's that play with Alan Horgan," he said. "*Adamant Eve.* It's a comedy."

"It was funny?"

"I thought so. But Mr. Ellman talked about it the way Mom talks about her soap operas, as if it was all very serious. I don't think he really enjoyed it."

"You and Ellman getting along all right?" his father asked.

Marsh shrugged. "I guess so," he said.

The television program was a talk show. An actress Marsh had never heard of before was explaining to the world at large why she would never dream of marrying the father of her child. He remembered what Donna had once said about a similar situation. "It's all right for some big name star who can afford to go ahead and have the baby and let somebody else take care of it. I mean what's she got to lose? But when you have parents or school or a job to think about—well, what are you supposed to do?"

"Our company might move out of town," Mr. Berger said gravely. "Don't say anything to your mother about it. I didn't tell her."

"When is it supposed to happen?" Marsh asked.

"No telling. It's still just a rumor really, but it's getting stronger every day. I'm waiting till it's official before I tell your mother about it. You know the way she carries on. No sense bringing that on if we can avoid it."

"What'll you do if it does happen?"

"What can I do? Get another job. It shouldn't be too hard. I've had a lot of experience. For four years I've been running the shipping department practically on my own, supervising three messengers and a truck driver. And before that I did shop work, so I'm all-round."

Mr. Berger lapsed into a silence shattered only by the sound of a television personality yawping on about the "wonderful frankness" of today's youth.

"When will you know if they're going to move or not?" Marsh asked.

"Some of the guys wanted to go down to the union tonight to get the representative to come find out about it one way or another," his father said. "In a way it could be good, because there's a provision in the contract against their becoming a runaway shop. If they did move out of the city they might have to give us a hell of a lot of severance pay before they went. Something like one week's salary for every year you worked for the company."

Mr. Berger took a heavy swallow from his beer can. "Of course, that wouldn't mean much to these kids who come in to work as messengers and don't stay more than a few months. But for someone like me it'd come in real handy." He pursed his lips and narrowed his eyes into a faraway, planning look. "It'd see us through until I get another job, anyway. And if I got one right away, then it would be a windfall that would help you when you're getting started in college."

Marsh felt he ought to say something like "Don't worry about me," but before he could get the words out his father asked him again how he was getting along with Ellman.

"Okay," Marsh answered.

"You *really* feel he's helping you?" his father asked.

Marsh shrugged. "Sometimes I wonder," he said. "For a while I didn't see how he could do me much good, really. He doesn't tie his work in with the classwork at all. Still, I have to admit he must have something going for him. Our history teacher gives us a quiz every Friday and I did better on the last few quizzes than I ever did before."

"That's the main thing," his father said. "As long as you get better in the subject, that proves he knows what he's doing."

Marsh grinned, shook his head and said nothing.

Mrs. Berger was washing dishes when Marsh came home from school Friday afternoon.

"Guess what?" Marsh said. "I'm going to be on the quiz team!"

"What's the quiz team?" his mother said.

"Something they're having at school. Did you ever see that program on television, 'Scholarship Quiz'?"

"No. It's a quiz program?"

"Yeah. They have it every Saturday afternoon."

Mrs. Berger stopped washing dishes. "You're going to be on television?" she said. "Marsh!"

She ran and put her arms around him. "When?" she asked. "Tell me! I have to call everybody!"

"No, no!" Marsh said. "It's not definite!"

"What do you mean, it's not definite? Are you going to be on television or not? You're getting me all excited for nothing."

"The *school* is going to be represented on television. They're trying to make up a team, and I might get to be on it."

His mother sat at the kitchen table. "What do you have to do to get on the team? What do you have to have?"

"They picked twelve kids," Marsh said. "Every afternoon we go down into the auditorium for quiz practice. We have a regular quiz session, just like the television program, with Mr. Reedy as moderator. Then, after three weeks, Mr. Reedy picks out the four students that will represent the school on television and four other kids to act as substitutes."

"And you're one of the ones."

"I'm one of the twelve, anyway."

"Marsh, I'm so proud of you."

"And listen to this. If you go on television and your team wins, you get five hundred dollars to help you toward college."

"Five hundred dollars!" Mrs. Berger was flabbergasted.

"And if your team wins the championship, you get a big scholarship."

It was too much for Mrs. Berger. "It's like the answer to a prayer," she said. "If you go on television and get a scholarship, you could go to any college you want. I can't believe it."

Marsh began pacing restlessly around the kitchen table.

"I can't get over it," he said. "They picked only six people from the senior class and I'm one of them!"

"Well, why shouldn't you be?" his mother asked. "I always knew you were a smart boy."

"Me?" Marsh said, his voice cracking into a laugh. It was not that he did not believe his mother, but rather that he wanted to hear her say more on the subject, to stretch out one of the all too few joyous moments they had together.

"Don't underestimate yourself," his mother said. "You got a good set of brains. You wouldn't believe it to hear me now, but when I was a girl in school, all my teachers thought highly of me. There was always brains in our family. All they needed was a chance to come out."

"But it's not just brains," Marsh said. "That's what Mr. Reedy told us. He said you could be the smartest guy in the world but if you don't get your finger on the button at the right moment you could still wash out. The knowledge is important, he said, but the game is mostly a matter of quick thinking and good reflexes."

"Whatever it is," his mother said, "you got what it takes."

"I just hope I don't wash out in the first eliminations."

"Not a chance," his mother said. "Hey, what am I sitting here talking for? Let me get to the telephone and call your Aunt Rona. And Mrs. Ferling."

Marsh's father took the news quietly.

"I guess I won't have to do much worrying about you," he said. "They seem to think highly of you up at that school."

"Well, some of my grades *have* improved lately," Marsh said. "And Mr. Reedy says I take more part in class discussions now than I used to."

"I'll bet Mr. Ellman was pleased to hear how well you're doing."

"Mr. Ellman?"

"You didn't tell him yet?"

"No. I . . . Dad, that's something I wanted to talk to you about."

"Ellman?"

"From now on, on top of everything else, I'm going to have quiz practice every day and—well, something's got to give somewhere and I was thinking maybe I could cut out the sessions with Mr. Ellman. What do you think?"

"I think it would be a very foolish thing to do."

"Why?"

Mr. Berger's expression was that of a man struggling to find the words to express something that he assumed was self-evident.

"Because it would be like—like biting the hand that feeds you."

"You think it's because of Mr. Ellman that I got chosen for the quiz team?"

"I don't know if it was or not," his father answered. "But you yourself said that since you've been working with Ellman your grades have improved and now you're picked out for something like this. I don't know if that's Ellman's doing or not, but he is part of the deal, part of the package. It's common sense not to rock the boat."

"In other words, I can't quit Ellman."

"I'm not telling you not to. All I'm saying is you'd be very foolish if you did. I mean this quiz business is all very nice and all that, but remember there's still that big test coming up, and if you ask me, the city colleges are a lot surer bet than any television scholarship."

"Okay," Marsh said. "You win."

Chapter 8

A few weeks after Ida's funeral, Norman called Ellman to ask if he wanted some tapes that Jacob had made.

"Tapes?" Ellman asked.

"They're just homemade recordings. I don't know what they sound like. Mom said once that she was thinking of having them copied professionally—amplified and all that—but I don't know if she ever did it. Anyway, we found a bunch of them the other day while we were going through her things and I thought you might like to have them."

"I would," Ellman said. "When can I get them?"

"The only reason I was hesitating to send them to you," Norman said, "was that neither Nathan nor I was sure whether or not you had a machine to play them on."

"I'll get one," Ellman said.

Norman's voice broke into a laugh. "I didn't expect you to go that far," he said.

"Norman, all I have left of Jacob's playing is that he is one of the people in the string section of my Contradini records. If there are any records of Jacob playing by himself, then I want them."

In spite of the decisive tone he had taken with Norman, it took two trips to the department store before Ellman could make up his mind to spend so much money on what his cautious mind kept telling him was just a foolish return to the past. He was helped to the final decision by the rationalization that these days a tape recorder might easily be considered a teaching aid. It might someday help him in his work with Marsh.

The tape recorder was delivered on Thursday. Ellman immediately called Norman and arranged to meet him on Friday and pick up the tapes from him. Now, with the six precious tapes in his hands, Ellman rushed home for an evening with Jacob.

The tapes were not marked as to selections, but as soon as he put the first of them on, Ellman was convinced that they had been worth all the trouble and expense he had gone through to secure them. The first tape was a recording of the *Kreutzer* Sonata. Listening to it was like having Jacob in the room with him again, playing at one of the home recitals as he had done so often in the past. Even the grumblings, the asides and the comments between movements and after the performances came across on the tape.

The second side of the third tape was full of old Hasidic melodies that took Ellman back to the days of Nonsch the fiddler. Ellman was totally lost in the past when a knock at the door brought him abruptly back to the present.

He hated to have the performance interrupted, but now that he had established a working relationship with the family downstairs, he had got into the habit of answering the door whenever he heard a knock.

"Mr. Berger," he said warmly. "Come right in."

Mr. Berger entered and took a seat. Ellman turned off the tape recorder and explained to his guest what he had been listening to.

"Oh, that was your *brother* playing?" Mr. Berger commented. "It must be wonderful to be able to play an instrument like that."

"Yes," Ellman agreed. "Unfortunately, Jacob was never as successful as he ought to have been, but to hear him play like that . . . Yes, that was indeed wonderful."

"Me, I wanted to take up the trumpet in school, but we never could afford it."

Ellman smiled.

"Listen to me talking about trumpets," Mr. Berger said. "When it comes to beautiful music, there's no comparing anything with a violin."

As if to close off all discussion of music, Ellman put the lid back on the tape recorder.

"I brought you some good news," Mr. Berger announced.

"About Marshall?" Ellman asked. The only "good" news he could imagine Mr. Berger bringing him about Marsh was that in some way Marsh had been accepted by a college and therefore would not have to take any more lessons with him. This, while it might be good news to Mr. Berger, would be a serious blow for Ellman.

"He would have come up and told you himself, but you know how kids are. He wanted to go right off and tell his girl. I told him I wanted to come up here myself anyway. It's been a long time since we had any kind of talk."

Ellman nodded.

"They picked him at school to try out for that television program 'Scholarship Quiz.' "

Ellman was shocked. This was justification beyond anything he could have dreamed of. Still, he was not certain he liked the idea.

"A quiz program?" he asked. "On television?"

"It's not certain that he's going to make it yet, but he was one of the kids picked to try out for it."

Mr. Berger repeated everything Marsh had told him about the quiz.

"I wish him every success," Ellman said cautiously. "I'm sure he'll do very well."

"I ought to thank you in a way, I guess," Mr. Berger said. "Like I told Marsh, even if he was picked out mostly for the subjects he's been doing all right in all along, I still think you must have had something to do with it."

In the circumstances, it was not hard for Ellman to look modest.

"What I've tried to teach Marshall more than anything else," he said, "is the art of concentration. Concentration and persistence. If he learns those two things, nothing at school will ever trouble him again."

"He *is* getting better marks on his history quizzes," Mr. Berger observed sagely.

After Mr. Berger had left, Ellman returned to his tape recordings. He wished now that Callahan had a telephone in his room. That not being the case, however, he determined to visit his friend the next evening.

Callahan was not at all pleased when Ellman told him about Marsh and the television quiz.

"You started out so full of the wonderful idea of teaching, of imparting knowledge," he said scornfully. "And where do you end up? Coaching a contestant on a quiz program."

"It's not like that at all," Ellman protested.

"You take knowledge and make a game out of it," Callahan insisted. "It's like that time I went to the Botanical Gardens in Brooklyn. The most beautiful sight I ever saw was the cherry blossoms in bloom there and instead of enjoying the beauty of it, all anybody could think of to do was to take pictures of it."

Ellman had heard of Callahan's visit to the cherry blossoms many times, but he did not see how it related to "Scholarship Quiz."

"It's the same approach. We have no capacity for just enjoying beauty. We have to do something about it. And the snap of the camera completes—or rather terminates—any experience of beauty we have. There! You've done something about it! Now you can forget it."

"Let's go to the Automat," Ellman said.

"You talk about the sacredness of knowledge," Callahan said. "But to your television friends, knowledge is like beauty is to the picture snappers—something you have to *do* something about. So what they do is make a competitive game of it. And instead of quarreling with that, instead of trying to talk the kid out of it, you stand there and take bows for helping him."

Callahan's bad humor persisted even after they had arrived at the Automat. In fact, it became worse there because of the presence of some teen-age kids in the corner who were playing their transistor radio so loud that it could be heard in the farthest reaches of the restaurant. No sooner had he and Ellman sat down at their table than Callahan announced his intention of shouting at the kids to turn the damned thing off.

"Stop behaving like a cranky old man," Ellman told him. "It's the kind of music the kids like. We ought to be interested in it."

"Oh, come off it," Callahan said. "Ever since this teaching project started you've been acting like you were some kind of a kid yourself. What would your brother have said about music like that?"

"Jacob would have said that it was interesting," Ellman asserted. "The only kind of music that Jacob disliked was electronic music."

Callahan, in his grouchy mood, started to dismiss this as an expedient fabrication of Ellman's but Ellman enlarged upon it.

"Jacob used to say that in music, the rhythm is the heartbeat and the melody is the breath. Electronic music, he said, is neither rhythmic nor melodic. It has no heart and it doesn't breathe. Just the right music for a world like ours."

The kids had risen en masse from their table and were slowly rocking their way to the door. The transistor did not let up for a moment.

"It's enough to make you sick," Callahan said in disgust. "Just a big jangle. Sounds like static. You can't even understand it."

The boy carrying the radio danced near Callahan. For a moment Ellman thought his friend was going to swing out and hit him.

"Everywhere you go you see them," Callahan said. "A pack of morons with their ears glued to that garbage."

After some horseplay at the revolving door, the kids passed out into the street and a calm settled over the restaurant, broken only by the sound of piped-in violins. The music now had a faintly discernible pulse and it breathed in a dreamy, quiet sort of way, but Ellman found it bloodless. *He* would have preferred to struggle awhile longer with the rock music.

"Is this stuff any better?" he asked Callahan.

"At least it gives you a chance to hear yourself think," Callahan said.

"Maybe that's why they listen to the other kind of music," Ellman suggested. "They don't want to think."

"You can say that again," Callahan said. "Pass me the sugar."

Ellman obliged. "You and I were taught to learn the lesson of history by studying the past," he said. "But they are learning from their own vision of the future. What have they got to look forward to anyway? Nuclear wars, a polluted atmosphere, an exploding population—"

"I don't think these kids have given five minutes' thought to any of those things in their whole lives," Callahan said.

"They don't have to think about it to be affected by it. It's in the air. Even with their ears glued to their radios, they learn about it. And what are they learning? They are learning to seize the moment and exploit it. Oh, I can understand about the transistors, all right."

"The only time I hear that kind of junk is in the morning when I have the radio on to get the time and the weather reports."

"To some people, transistors are not so much a means of pleasure as a necessity," Ellman said.

"You don't go to work in the mornings anymore, I can see that," Callahan said.

"What's that got to do with it?"

"That's when you see the kids on their way to school. Most of them are still half asleep. They wander around the street till all hours of the night and then in the mornings they drag themselves to school half dead. You see them in the subway copying their homework from other kids. In the subway yet!"

"They're not *all* like that."

"No. There's got to be a couple of kids that actually do their homework so that the others can have somebody to copy from. And you'll get one or two now and then opening their books to actually get some studying done."

"On the subway?" Ellman was intrigued. "I wonder if Marshall does that."

Ellman walked Callahan back to his house.

"I'll see you next week," Ellman said.

"Yeah, next week," Callahan agreed. "You can tell me what progress you're making with the quiz kid."

When he was halfway up the steps to his house, Callahan turned and gave Ellman his benediction.

"You're supposed to be helping this kid," he said. "Whatever he wants and however he has to go about getting it, let's at least hope that he ends up with something better than this."

Chapter 9

"Now I'm not going to give you a pep talk," Mr. Reedy said. "You all know why you have been chosen, and you all know that only four of you are going to be on the team."

Marsh looked around him at the competition. There were really only nine he had to contend with. Automatically he yielded to Foster Gilson and Dennis Kite. Gilson was class president, a brilliant and popular kid; Kite was editor of the school paper. There would be no chance to unseat either of them from the team.

Of the nine other competitors, only two were seniors. Danny Lensman was bright, but he was also on the shy side. That would make him hesitate a bit before pushing the button that would call attention to himself, so Marsh had an edge there. Jerry Tynan, on the other hand, was a mine of self-confidence, but then Jerry's store of knowledge was a bit shaky. Marsh had known Jerry to argue with a teacher on a fact about which everybody but Jerry knew that he was absolutely wrong. So unless Marsh ran into an unusual run of bad questions right at the start, he could count on Jerry's eliminating himself. The first time Jerry started to quibble about a decision, he would be off the team permanently.

Of the others Marsh recognized only one—Harmon Grochuk, a junior. He was a star on the basketball team, but Marsh knew nothing of his scholastic achievements. The rest were lowerclassmen. Two of them were black, though, and Marsh wondered if Mr. Reedy might be influenced in favor of one of them, figuring that it would be an advantage to have an integrated team.

"How many of you have watched 'Scholarship Quiz' on television?" Mr. Reedy asked.

The only ones who did not raise their hands were Marsh and one of the black kids.

"Then most of you know how it works," Mr. Reedy summarized. "For the rest, I don't think I need to tell you that while we are working on this project it will be to your advantage to watch the program every week."

Mr. Reedy picked out eight of the ten students who watched the program and divided them into two teams of four each.

"Each school is represented by a team of four members," Mr. Reedy explained. "You on the right are Team A and you on the left are Team B. Now let me explain to you all what we're going to be doing for the next few weeks. First, we are going to try all possible combinations of teams because we want to see how all of you function as team members. We don't just want the best four individuals. What we are trying to put together is the best possible team. Bear that in mind. Also, I want you to know now that nobody will be eliminated until the first two weeks of practice are up."

Foster Gilson raised his hand.

"You said the best team members would be selected," he said. "But on the program they score on an individual basis also. The first round just puts one person from each team against each other and the second round takes only two from each side."

"True," Mr. Reedy conceded. "But the heaviest points are in round three where all four team members work together."

Mr. Reedy distributed mimeographed forms to the four students who were not acting as contestants, and assigned each one of them two contestants whom he was to grade.

Foster Gilson raised his hand again. "What if someone responds to a question but the response is neither correct nor incorrect?"

This got a laugh, which Gilson did not expect. He was not the sort of kid who broke up his classes with irrelevancies. Instead of enjoying the laughter he had provoked, he seemed to be upset by it.

Marsh nudged Danny Lensman, who was sitting next to him. "Gilson's afraid Reedy'll eliminate him as a cutup."

"What I meant was suppose the response is a false response. One of those cases where you feel you know the answer but you can't get it off the tip of your tongue, so that instead of answering once you've given the signal, you snap your fingers or slap your head, things like that."

"Anything but a correct response is to be marked incorrect," Mr. Reedy said.

This time it was Dennis Kite who raised his hand. "Do the incorrect answers count against you?" he wanted to know. "Which is worse, answering wrong or not answering at all?"

Mr. Reedy's answer was an evasive comment that the best thing to do would be to answer correctly.

Someone else wanted to know how they were to signal. On the television program they used a buzzer to indicate that they knew the answer.

"For the present," Mr. Reedy said, "we'll just use a clap of the hands."

There was some more quibbling about what to do in case of a tie and suppose somebody clapped louder than somebody else, but Mr. Reedy overrode all this with the statement that he was to be the judge and that in all cases the decision of the judge was to be considered final.

"The first round is the individual competition," he said.

"One person from each team. I think we'll take Mr. Gilson from Team A and Mr. Kite from Team B."

Class President versus Newspaper Editor. Marsh smiled.

"I'll call out the questions," Mr. Reedy said. "As soon as you think you know the answer, clap your hands. Lensman, you make note of Mr. Gilson's reactions. Richards, you keep track of Mr. Kite's. Just write down which questions your contestant responds to and whether he gets them right or not. Berger, you'll be the official scorekeeper for this round. You just keep the points—ten gained for each correct answer; ten lost for each incorrect answer."

Marsh considered calling Mr. Reedy's attention to the fact that he was one of those who had never watched the program, but he quashed the thought. The directions were simple enough.

Mr. Reedy took a sheaf of papers off a table at the front of the room.

"Some of the questions we're using are actual questions used on the program in the past," he said. "The rest I made up myself."

Mr. Reedy had set a high standard by beginning with Gilson and Kite. The first round was quick and tense, each of the contestants determined to prove himself worthy to represent the school. Gilson and Kite were the best of friends and each seemed aware that, in some unspoken way, Mr. Reedy was depending on them to show all the others just exactly what was expected of them.

The rivalry was sharp and it was seldom that Mr. Reedy got to finish a question before one or the other of the contestants had clapped his hands. At one point Gilson, forgetting to clap his hands at all, shouted out an answer. Kite thereupon clapped his hands, gave the same answer and received ten points for it.

Marsh wished he had not been made scorekeeper because it

made it more difficult for him to concentrate on the format of the game itself and the nature of the questions being asked. He was trying to participate in the game as actively as either of the two contestants and yet found himself constantly distracted by the need to keep adding and subtracting by tens. If Danny Lensman had not been saddled with the job of keeping track of Gilson, Marsh would have asked him to help with the scoring.

Gilson clapped his hands loudly before Mr. Reedy had time to complete the last question.

"The *Divine Comedy*," he said confidently.

"Wrong," Mr. Reedy announced. "I repeat the question."

The boys had been clapping their hands so loudly that the soreness in their palms had already become a subject for laughter. When Mr. Reedy completed the last question, Kite tapped one palm very lightly with the fingers of the other hand. Gilson, who knew what the correct answer should be, was already laughing.

Kite took a deep breath, as though the answer he had to give would be a very long one.

"Dante," he said briefly.

"Correct," said Mr. Reedy. "Scorekeeper?"

There was a brief round of applause for the contestants. When it was finished, Marsh got up to announce the scores.

"Gilson eighty, Kite seventy."

There was an immediate chorus of protest.

"Ninety," everyone was shouting. "Ninety."

Mr. Reedy looked away from Marsh. "Ninety for whom?" he asked.

"Gilson."

"Scorekeeper, there seems to be some difference of opinion."

Marsh shook his head. "All I can say is I make it out Gilson eighty, Kite seventy."

With so many shouting him down, there could be no question but that Marsh was wrong. Mr. Reedy accepted the group's score and chose the next two contestants. Marsh reached over and asked Danny Lensman to let him have Gilson's sheet for a minute.

Gilson's sheet reflected ten correct responses and one incorrect.

"It's not right," Marsh said. "You didn't keep it right."

It was Marsh's own chagrin that had caused him to come down so heavily on Danny. When he saw the deep flush of confusion that suffused the other boy's face, he was a little ashamed of himself.

"There's a mistake in it," he said to Danny in a tone that was supposed to convey apology as well as explanation.

"What's the trouble over there?" Mr. Reedy called.

Marsh stood up.

"I was checking the sheet to see where I went wrong," he said. "The sheet shows ninety points for Gilson also." He glanced briefly at Danny. He hated to embarrass the guy, but right was right.

"The sheet's wrong too," Marsh announced.

A groaning chorus burst from the group and Marsh heard someone mutter, "Everybody's wrong but Berger."

Mr. Reedy, however, was open to explanations.

"The sheet shows one incorrect answer," Marsh said. "But he actually gave two."

Marsh expected to hear another protest at this, but instead there was silence. It was an ominous silence, as if everyone in the room were quietly waiting for Marsh to step into a trap.

"There was the last question," he said slowly, "about Dante and the *Divine Comedy*. And then there was the first one, about the Treaty of Paris."

"Doesn't count," Kite said.

There was something doubly shameful about having Kite

point out his error to him, since Kite was the one who stood to gain by having Gilson's score reduced a bit.

"He called out about the Treaty of Paris without clapping his hands," Kite explained. "So it doesn't really count as an incorrect answer. You just don't count it at all."

"I didn't know that," Marsh said. "I don't watch the program."

He thought of announcing that he was sorry, but rejected this on the grounds that it would make it look as though he were trying too hard. He sat down slowly as the next match began.

He glanced ruefully at Danny Lensman. He felt bad about that part of it.

"It's a good thing you kept careful track," he said, "or I'd never have known where I went wrong."

But Danny stared straight ahead of him, paying no attention to Marsh.

The practice session ended after Round Three, in which the teams worked as teams. Gilson's team won.

"Those of you who did not get a chance today will serve as contestants next time," Mr. Reedy announced.

When Marsh's father asked him that night about the practice session, Marsh said, "Well, I wouldn't build my hopes up on my making the team."

His father gave him a pep talk.

"Tell me," Ellman said during their session the next evening. "On your way home from school, do you take out a book and study in the subway?"

"Sometimes," Marsh said.

"I think it might be better if you didn't do that."

Marsh uttered a youthful sound of surprised protest.

"If you feel it's a good practice," the tutor went on, "you can continue to do it in the mornings. But in the afternoons there is something else I want you to try. Instead of opening a book, just sit back and try to remember as much as you can of what went on in class that day. In the beginning, do it with just one class—history, for example. Try to recall everything that was covered. If it helps, you can imagine me there asking you questions."

The first time Marsh tried this, the results were excellent. He became so absorbed in recalling details of Mr. Tasker's discussion of Reconstruction that he went past his station and had to take another train back. The second time, however, he found it fatiguing. Each time he made himself remember the history class, it was only to laugh again at Jerry Tynan's silly joke about the carpetbaggers. When he finally got home that afternoon, he realized that he had spent most of his time recalling Jerry's best jokes and daydreaming about Jerry's sister Barbara.

"You mustn't *let* yourself be distracted," Ellman told him when Marsh confessed his difficulties. "That's why I told you to imagine me there with you."

Ellman decided to hear Marsh describe one class at each of their sessions.

These descriptions soon became a nightmare for Marsh. Ellman played a much more active part in them than he had during the history narrative, asking countless questions and pressing for more details. Nevertheless, Marsh found cause for hope in them, since they brought Ellman's lessons into alignment with his classroom work. At the same time, Marsh was beginning to feel that the time he spent with Ellman might be put to better use if he prepared for the quiz.

"By the way," Marsh said as he was leaving Ellman's one Monday night. "I won't be able to make Friday's session. They're having a parents' night at the school and my parents will probably want to go."

"Probably?" Ellman repeated. "You mean you haven't told them yet?"

Marsh shrugged.

"Is it just for parents?" Ellman asked.

"Do you want to come?"

"If you're sure it will be all right."

"I'll ask them at school tomorrow and let you know."

At quiz practice the next day, Marsh's work in the individual round was quite good. He scored nine correct responses and no incorrect ones, but it was not a success he could feel secure in. Somehow he could not shake the feeling that he had just run into a lucky series of questions. He found himself clapping his hands and coming up with answers even before he was consciously sure he had understood the questions.

Mr. Reedy had begun the session by reminding all the students of the parents' night and telling them that while all parents would be welcome, the parents of students in this group would be particularly welcome. Marsh took this to mean that the appearance of their parents might have some bearing on their possible selection as members of the final team.

At the end of the session two of the candidates went up to Mr. Reedy to explain to him why their parents would not be able to make it that night. Mr. Reedy looked over their heads, however, and called to Marsh.

"Berger," he called. "I want to see you before you go."

Mr. Reedy explained to the two anxious students that of course no parent could be obliged to come to a parents' night, but that he himself would like very much to have an opportunity to meet the parents of *all* his team members.

"*Your* parents are coming that night, aren't they?" he asked Marsh after the others had gone.

"I don't know," Marsh said. "To tell the truth, I haven't even told them about it yet."

"You haven't? Why not?"

"No reason," Marsh said, shrugging. "I guess they'll come."

"I'll be honest with you, Berger," Mr. Reedy said. "You've

been surprising me with your work in the quiz. You're doing much better than I expected."

"Talk about surprises," Marsh said. "I was surprised I was even picked to have a chance for something like this."

"Why should you be surprised?" the teacher asked. "I've seen your record. You've been doing quite well in most of your courses."

"Have you seen my history marks?" Marsh smiled ruefully, but Mr. Reedy did not acknowledge the humor.

"Yes, I have," he said, "and Mr. Tasker tells me they've been improving quite a bit lately."

Mr. Reedy began gathering up his papers.

"On a quiz like this, you have to understand that what we want is a well-rounded student, one who can answer questions in many fields. By the same token, we don't expect to get anyone who is expert in anything. You were chosen because your general average is good, your marks in mathematics are excellent and you seem to have the kind of spirit that a game like this calls for."

Marsh grinned.

"Don't start taking any bows yet," Mr. Reedy added hastily. He swept the last few pieces of paper off the desk and indicated that he was ready to go. Marsh preceded him out of the room, knowing that Mr. Reedy would have to lock it behind them.

They started walking down the hallway.

Mr. Reedy paused at the main entrance.

"About Friday," he said to Marsh. "You will tell your parents?"

Marsh hesitated. "I suppose so."

Mr. Reedy seemed amused. "What does that mean?" he asked. "Do you have something else to do that night?"

Marsh's mind was on getting out the door, but he could not ignore Mr. Reedy.

"I usually have a session with the tutor on Fridays," he muttered.

Mr. Reedy did not hear him clearly.

"What was that?" the teacher said.

"Nothing," Marsh answered. "I'll be there on Friday."

Mr. Reedy frowned. He had the bearing of a teacher who feels he has got off on the wrong foot with a student.

"Good afternoon then," he said.

Marsh turned from the doorway and called:

"Mr. Reedy, is Friday night just for parents, or would it be all right to bring someone else along too? A friend of the family, say."

"Of course," Mr. Reedy said. "Bring anyone you wish."

Marsh told his parents at the dinner table. His father said it was kind of short notice and his mother said of course they'd come.

"I mentioned it to Mr. Ellman last night," Marsh said. "He said to see if it was all right with the school for him to come too. I have to go upstairs tonight and tell him it's okay."

"Of all the nerve!" Mrs. Berger said.

Mr. Berger looked admiringly at Marsh. "It sounds like a good idea," he said. "I'm sure Mr. Ellman will be pleased."

"Over my dead body Mr. Ellman will be pleased," said Mrs. Berger. "It's not bad enough all the neighbors know about it. Now you want to take him to the school so all your teachers and friends there can get a load of the kind of tutor your father picked out."

"I didn't tell them he was my tutor," Marsh said. "Besides, there's always the possibility that he might not even want to come."

"Why shouldn't he?" asked Mr. Berger. "He's the one who asked about it, isn't he?"

"He's kind of funny sometimes," Marsh said. "When you come down to it, you never know how he'll react."

"So don't let him react," Mrs. Berger said. "Don't tell him."

Mr. Berger pushed his chair back from the table. "Now that's the kind of thing I just don't understand," he said. "You were against Ellman at the start. All right, I could understand that. He was an unknown quantity then. But now you've seen the way he's helped Marsh with the history, the way his grades have picked up—"

"He hasn't helped *that* much," Marsh said.

"There, what did I tell you?" said Mrs. Berger.

Mr. Berger came down on Marsh. "Make up your mind," he said. "First he's good for you and then he's not. Which is it?"

It was a question Marsh had been asking himself for quite some time now. Even as he tried to explain it to his father, he was still groping for the answer himself.

"He helps me," he said. "But not in the way I expected."

"Your grades are better, you're on the quiz team—"

Marsh saw an opportunity to change the subject on a point of fact. "I'm not on the team yet," he said. "They don't make the final choice till Monday."

"You're closer to it than you expected to be," his father said. "If that's not Ellman's doing, whose is it?"

"I'm on the team—or rather I'm among the candidates—because of the same subjects I was doing all right in before Ellman started. I talked to Mr. Reedy about it today and he said—"

"Never mind Mr. Reedy," his father said. "Talk about Ellman."

"He said it already," Mrs. Berger said. "Ellman is not helping him."

"He *is* helping me," Marsh insisted.

His parents looked at one another.

"He helps me in a general sort of way," Marsh explained. "But when it comes down to the particulars, in terms of the kind of questions they ask on an examination, I don't really see how he helps me at all."

His father spoke gently. "Marsh," he said, "the whole idea of Ellman is to help you do better on an exam."

His mother spoke less gently. "If he doesn't do that, why waste the time?"

"He *helps*," Marsh said. "I don't mean to say he doesn't. I know he helps. I feel it. It's just I don't see how."

His father was satisfied with that and his mother decided to let it pass.

"So are you going to ask him for Friday or not?" his father asked.

Marsh thought about it for a moment.

"I'll ask him," he said.

Ellman took his suit and topcoat to the cleaners, sent three shirts to the laundry, bought himself a new tie and a new pair of shoes and arrived early at Callahan's in his eagerness to tell him the news.

"Parents' night?" Callahan said sourly. "What are you going to do at a parents' night? Are you some kind of a parent now?"

"It's just a get-together at the school. A sort of PTA thing except they don't have PTA at that school."

"What do I know about the PTA?" Callahan asked.

Ellman was aware of the existence of Callahan's three children, but he could not tell from the tone of his friend's voice whether he was bragging about having escaped the farther reaches of parenthood or regretting the opportunities he had missed.

"The parents get to meet the teachers," Ellman explained, "and the teachers get to meet the parents, and everybody gets to understand one another a little better."

"I still don't see how *you* fit in," Callahan said. "Are you just supposed to be going along for the ride?"

"It will be useful for me to see the school Marsh goes to and the kind of teachers he has."

"All right," Callahan said. "Go to the meeting. Have a

nice time. Meet all the teachers. Maybe you can even pick up a few pointers."

"Tell me about the mnemonics poem," Ellman said. "How is it coming along?"

"None of that," Callahan said. "Tell me about the lessons. What do you two really *do* during your time together?"

Ellman did not want to discuss the content of his lessons. It was too much like bragging about the cake before you even took it out of the oven. By way of creating a diversionary action, he suggested that it was time they went for their coffee.

"Let's go someplace different tonight," Ellman said. "I feel like treating. How about that place on Seventh Avenue?"

"I'm not going to sit up all night with a stomachache just because you think you've got something to celebrate," Callahan said. "We'll go to the Automat and I'll have my regular coffee and cake."

All the way to the Automat and through most of their coffee, Callahan kept asking Ellman about the curriculum he was using with Marsh. It was quite a while before Ellman began to understand why his friend was so persistent and so testy. Callahan, he concluded at last, was casting himself in the role of an inquisitorial teacher at the parents' night. It was an implicit way of warning Ellman that he had better be prepared to answer some pretty stiff questions.

Ellman decided to stop fighting it.

"I've been thinking of starting him on speed reading," he said.

"What the hell do you know about speed reading?" Callahan demanded. "You take a quarter of an hour to read a picture caption."

Ellman smiled at the exaggeration.

"I have several books on the subject at home," he said. "I know the techniques involved. In fact, there's more than one method and I'm familiar with quite a few of them."

"But are you one yourself? A speed reader, I mean."

There was some critic's line about not having to eat the whole egg in order to tell it was rotten. Ellman tried to work out a paraphrase of it that would fit the present situation.

"You're not, are you?" Callahan persisted.

"What does that have to do with it?" Ellman said. "I don't have to use the techniques on myself in order to know they're good."

"You have no experience learning it and you have no experience teaching it," Callahan pointed out. "You know the destination and you know which road to take, but you don't know the pitfalls and potholes along that road."

"I haven't done badly so far, have I?" Ellman said.

"That's no argument."

"It's the *only* argument. The painting is the painter's argument. The statue is the sculptor's argument. And Marshall is my argument. My argument and my justification."

Chapter 10

Mrs. Berger drew the line at allowing Ellman to accompany them to the school.

"Tell him where it is and how to get there," she told Marsh. "Let him find his way himself."

Mr. Berger protested that such a course could only hurt the old man's feelings.

"Good," said Mrs. Berger. "If his feelings are hurt, maybe he won't want to come."

"But how is it going to look? What kind of people is he going to think we are?"

Mrs. Berger did not care what kind of people Ellman thought they were, but she seized the opportunity to give Mr. Berger another breakdown on what kind of person she thought Ellman was.

"It's bad enough having to be seen at the school with him. I am not going to walk through my own neighborhood with him."

No argument prevailed, and in the end Mr. Berger told Marsh to break the news as tactfully as he could to Ellman.

"Tell him we'd like to have him come along, but that we won't be around the house that night."

Marsh shook his head. "Suppose he sees us when we're leaving?" he said.

Mrs. Berger spoke up again. "I'm not sneaking out of my own house just on account of him."

"You won't have to lie to him," Mr. Berger said. "You and your mother can meet me after work and we'll eat out. We'll go to a restaurant and then straight from there to the school."

"I don't like it," Mrs. Berger said. "The kind of food you get in restaurants these days. I'd rather have dinner in my own kitchen where you don't have to rush—"

"The food'll be all right and we'll have plenty of time," Mr. Berger said.

"I still don't like it. The first time in years we get to go to a restaurant and it has to be because of *him*." She made an expressive gesture toward the ceiling, raising her head, stretching her neck and returning to normal in a lightning-quick motion that made Marsh think of a bird he had seen once in a nature film.

"It's not just on account of him," Mr. Berger said. "It's a big night for Marsh too. We'll do it for him."

Bowling Green High School was located in the West Eighties. Ellman had little difficulty finding the building but, once outside it, he did have something of a problem finding an open door. He made nearly a complete circuit of the school before he came to a door decorated with hand-painted signs that informed him with pastel gaiety that it was PARENTS' NIGHT and that he was to ENTER HERE.

The vestibule smelled of wax and wood polish. Ellman surmised that the school had been primped up that afternoon but that it had not been properly ventilated afterward, so that now all the cleaning smells hung in the air, mysteriously blending with one another into a staleness that reminded him not so much of his school days as of the evenings he used to pass in the local movie house in the days before television.

There were several people in the lobby and Ellman made a

quick rule-of-thumb distinction between them. The people with their coats on were parents and the people without coats must be faculty. As he approached a group of parents, the smells of cleaning were dissipated into the heavy, sweet scents of perfume and toilet water.

He stopped near the parents and looked around him, wondering if the Bergers were there already. He did not catch sight of them along either corridor. It was possible, of course, that they might have gone to Marsh's home room, but he decided to wait a moment or two more before checking that out.

There was a bulletin board a short distance up the corridor. Ellman walked to it, expecting to find classroom schedules, an honor roll and maybe even a collection of drawings made by the students.

Once he had begun to walk up the hallway, he noticed that there was not only one bulletin board, but several, and that most of them were covered with pictures, described as an exhibition of photographs by the members of the Bowling Green High School Camera Club.

Cityscapes. Arty photographs of bridge suspension cables. Rooftop studies of smog. Geometric arrangements of iron railings and staircases. It bothered Ellman at first that there were so few people in the pictures, and that even these were not photographed directly. They had sneaked in, in a sense, their reflections being caught in the plate-glass windows of stores or on the shiny facades of the buildings.

There were faces in the next set of pictures, however, although they met with little approval from the couple standing next to Ellman. The pictures were all of derelicts. One was sprawled in a doorway. Another, covered with newspapers, was stretched out in an alley. A third was settled on a park bench. Ellman smiled as he studied the pictures. Apparently the photographer was rather on the timid side, since all his subjects happened to be asleep when he was taking their pictures.

"I don't know what people want to take pictures of things like that for," a man standing near him said.

"Human interest," his wife explained.

The man laughed. "If that's human," he said, "I'm not interested."

Next came a collection of automobile parts. Studies of fenders and hub caps and a distorted picture of an automobile's interior that made it look as big as Ellman's living room.

"I don't get it," the man said. "What's it supposed to mean?"

"Nothing," his wife said. "They're just pictures."

"Who needs a picture of a headlight?"

"I don't know," his wife said, shrugging. "They probably just want to show that the kids can take all kinds of pictures. Maybe someday this kid will get into advertising, taking pictures of cars."

The exhibition at the end of the corridor was getting the most attention. They were pictures of an Italian wedding. In the center was a stiff, traditional picture of the bride and groom, looking lifeless and typical. Surrounding that were pictures of the reception. The mother of the bride stuffing a fat face with a cheese concoction that dribbled down her chin. A couple of desiccated crones sitting on high-backed chairs against the wall. Children in party hats throwing candy at one another. The groom singing with his buddies.

"Now that's what I call human interest," the man ahead of Ellman said.

"Glorified snapshots," his wife answered. "They're good, though."

In the corner, one man was explaining earnestly to another, "It's a matter of cropping and printing to bring out the highlights. Good photographs are not just taken, they're made."

"The way they're dancing, it could even be a Jewish wedding," a woman said.

Ellman stepped away from the photographs and imagined himself trying to explain the exhibition to Callahan. "It was not like your cherry blossoms at all," he would say. "They were not trying to record something, they were trying to say something. But as to *what* they were trying to say, your guess is as good as mine. They go from abstractions to caricatures. Either nothing is happening at all or too much is happening. Any row of objects is decorated with the title 'Perspectives' or 'Symmetry' and any picture of people not looking straight at the camera is called 'Human Interest.' They see with other people's vision and reality becomes just a series of potentially good pictures. Somehow they've lost track of whatever it is that makes the pictures good."

Aloud Ellman said, "Maybe it is like the cherry blossoms, after all."

There was a man by the staircase who was not wearing a topcoat. Ellman asked him where room 302 was.

"Is that your son's home room?" the man asked.

"Yes," Ellman said.

"Before the home room visits, we're asking everyone to assemble in the auditorium for a short while. Just one flight down on this staircase."

Mr. Berger told his wife to meet him at the subway station rather than right at the job itself. It was five years since his wife had last met him at the job, but Mr. Berger still remembered the occasion. Their electric bill had been neglected and Mrs. Berger had to come up on payday and get money to pay the bill before the day was out.

Mr. Berger was never quite sure whether she had picked on the messenger first or the messenger had picked on her. All he was certain of was that when he came out after leaving the day's tickets in the front office, there was a verbal battle going on between the two of them, in the course of which she told the messenger that his people didn't have any respect for their betters and the messenger called her a Jew bitch. It was an ugly scene and Mr. Berger had no wish to have it repeated. Nor did he want a replay of the weeks that followed, during which she made a practice of asking him, each time he mentioned the job, if "that kid" was still working there.

It got worse when he made the mistake of offering to get Marsh a summer job there.

"Over my dead body," his wife said. "There's lots of jobs he could get where he wouldn't have to work with trash like that."

The offending messenger had long since left by then, but this did nothing to change Mrs. Berger's mind.

"Anytime Marsh needs a job," she said, "I got friends and relatives who can get him one. I don't want him running messages for that cheap outfit you work for."

So they met two blocks away from Mr. Berger's job. And Mrs. Berger was almost an hour late getting there.

"One time!" she said to Marsh as soon as she arrived. "One time you couldn't stay home awhile instead of rushing out again as soon as you got home from school."

"What happened?" Marsh said.

She addressed her husband. "Couldn't you tell him this morning to stay home after he got back from school this afternoon so that we could go together?" she said.

"I *said* I'd wait if you wanted me to," Marsh protested.

"You *said*," his mother repeated scornfully. "After you left, I couldn't find anything. My purse, anything. I even had to go out to the store to buy white shoe polish."

"I asked you if you wanted anything," Marsh said.

"I didn't know if I wanted anything or not. You should have stayed around and been there in *case* I wanted anything."

"Well, look, we wasted enough time already," Mr. Berger said. "Let's at least get to the restaurant."

"I feel so rotten now," Mrs. Berger said. "I'm half a mind I don't want to go."

Mr. Berger overrode this feeble objection and they moved on to a small fast-food restaurant where they each had hot roast beef sandwiches with mashed potatoes and string beans.

By the time they got to the school, the principal was making a speech in the auditorium, welcoming the parents and friends.

"There's Mr. Ellman," Marsh whispered. "Over there by Danny Lensman."

"Never mind Mr. Ellman," his mother said. "Where is this Mr. Whatsisname that's in charge of the quiz?"

As soon as the principal had finished his address, Mrs. Berger headed straight for Mr. Reedy. Unfortunately, another couple got to him first. When Mrs. Berger turned to her husband to comment on their bad luck, she noticed that Marsh was not with them.

"I sent him to get Ellman," Mr. Berger explained.

"You had to do that now?" Mrs. Berger whispered between clenched teeth.

"Well, he's supposed to be with us. We invited him. We can't ignore him, can we? Besides, what difference does it make?"

"In front of the regular teachers, maybe," his wife said enigmatically, "but not in front of the quiz teacher."

Ellman arrived with Marsh. "How do you do?" he said.

"You know my wife, don't you?" Mr. Berger asked.

"How do you do?" Mrs. Berger said coldly.

"I believe the principal said the homeroom teachers should all be in their classrooms now," Ellman said.

Mr. Berger opened his mouth to say something, but it was Mrs. Berger's voice that was heard.

"Good," she said. "You two go up there and we'll join you in a couple of minutes."

"But shouldn't we all stay together?" Marsh asked.

Mr. Berger was a good judge of how far his wife could be pushed. "You and Mr. Ellman go upstairs now," he told Marsh. "We'll come along later."

As soon as Marsh and the tutor were out of sight, Mrs. Berger stepped between Mr. Reedy and the tall lady who had been talking to him.

"You're Mr. Reedy?" she said. "I'm Mrs. Berger. Marshall Berger's mother."

The tall lady gave a start. She recovered quickly, however, and smiled.

"I mustn't take up all your time," she said to Mr. Reedy. "I'm off to room 213."

"Good-bye, Mrs. Gilson," Mr. Reedy said. "It was nice meeting you."

"Phil, come and meet Mr. Reedy. This is my husband."

"How do you do," Mr. Reedy said.

"Pleased to meet you," said Mr. Berger.

"Marsh has been telling us about this quiz he's in. I can't tell you how excited we are. We can't wait to see him on TV."

The teacher had not arrived in room 302 yet, so Marsh and Ellman linked up with Danny Lensman and his parents. Marsh introduced Ellman as a friend of the family.

"I think we sat next to you downstairs," Mrs. Lensman said, recognizing Ellman. "We didn't know who you were, though."

When Mr. and Mrs. Berger came up, they too were introduced to the Lensmans.

Mrs. Berger greeted Danny warmly.

"You're in the quiz too, aren't you?"

"We're very proud of Danny," Mrs. Lensman said. "He's going to Syracuse University in the fall."

Mrs. Berger's face fell.

"Marsh hasn't decided where he's going to go yet," she said.

"I'm trying to get into City College," Marsh said.

Mr. Berger put his hand on Marsh's shoulder.

"It's about all we can afford," he explained.

"Why don't you get a state loan?" Mrs. Lensman said. "That's what Danny did."

"I don't like the idea of getting into debt," Mrs. Berger said.

"But they have marvelous terms," Mrs. Lensman said. "You don't have to pay for years and years. Danny, what was the name of that counselor you told us about?"

"Mr. Davis."

"That's the one. See Mr. Davis. He'll tell you just what to do."

Marsh chuckled and paused before delivering his next line. "It was Mr. Davis who suggested I try City College," he said.

Danny and Ellman were the only ones who smiled. The others looked slightly embarrassed.

"Anyway," Mrs. Berger said, "if Marsh wins a scholarship on the quiz program, then we won't have to worry about finding a free college for him."

Marsh was angry and embarrassed at the same time.

"I've told you a thousand times they haven't even picked the team members yet," he said.

Danny, in his embarrassment for Marsh, had looked off toward the doorway.

"Here comes Mr. Foster," he announced.

Everyone moved toward the doorway to meet the teacher.

Ellman was pleased at being presented as a friend of the family rather than as a tutor, having been troubled by Callahan's doubts about how Marsh's teachers might react to what they would consider his amateur interference. So he went along with the concealment. It gave him an opportunity to see without being seen, in a sense. When they were leaving the school, the Bergers accepted an invitation from the Lensmans to join them for a hamburger at the corner restaurant. As they were sitting around the table, Mrs. Lensman made a polite inquiry about Ellman and that gentleman, now that they were safely away from the school, felt free to tell her that he "helped Marshall a little bit with his schoolwork."

"You *tutor* him," Mrs. Lensman said. "It's for the quiz, is it?"

There was knowing mockery in Danny Lensman's eyes.

"He helps me with English and American history," Marsh explained. "It's for the S.A.T. test. I won't get into City College unless I score pretty high on it."

Every time Marsh made any kind of reference to City College, however oblique, Mrs. Berger felt obliged to say something about "Scholarship Quiz." This time it was Mr. Lensman who answered her.

"It's really none of my business," he said, "but I wouldn't count too heavily on that if I were you. Remember, this is a competition, a quiz, and in a quiz anything can happen. More than anything else, it's a matter of luck."

"Exactly," said Ellman.

Marsh could have predicted that Ellman would begin sounding off about now. All he needed was to get that first cup of coffee in him.

"To win in a contest is an accomplishment," he was saying, "but it's not necessarily an accomplishment of knowledge. Too many other factors are allowed to interfere. The nerves and the emotions become involved. It is not so much a matter of acquiring or even using knowledge as—"

Ellman stopped in midsentence, as though what he had been saying was something that had just occurred to him, and he wanted to think some more about it before going on.

"Yes?" said Mr. Lensman.

". . . as of storing the knowledge one already possesses in such a way as to make it immediately available to one."

Ellman lapsed into an oracular silence. Mrs. Berger cast an angry glance at him and then smiled at Mr. Lensman.

"Anyway," she said, "we can always hope, can't we?"

"The trouble with memory systems," said Ellman, "is that they are not memory systems at all, but *memorizing systems*."

This had the sickly smell of a prepared remark. Marsh looked at his father and Mr. Berger glanced shamefacedly at Mr. Lensman. Mrs. Berger saw it as a justification of her efforts to keep Ellman away from the affair.

Ellman went on. "They are not ways of helping you recall things you've known and forgotten, but ways of helping you to learn things in the future. What I want is a memory system that will open up the treasures of the subconscious."

The last phrase had a flat, stale sound even to Marsh.

"Is that how you're tutoring Marsh?" Mr. Lensman asked pleasantly. "You use a memory system?"

"No," Ellman said. "I considered it, of course, but there wasn't time to adapt one to our purposes."

"You're familiar with the technique, then?" Mr. Lensman said.

"I have several books on the subject at home," Ellman said. "Some of them, of course, are only fit subject for laughter, but they all have at least the germ of an idea."

Now that Mr. Lensman's inquiries had given a touch of legitimacy to the topic, Mr. Berger felt free to confess that he had always been fascinated by "those advertisements that say they can give you a push-button memory," although he had no idea how any of the courses worked.

"I'd like to get a look at some of those books you were talking about," he told Ellman.

"It's getting late," Mrs. Berger said, before Ellman could answer. "Saturday or no Saturday, we all have to get up tomorrow so we might as well be on our way now."

Chapter 11

Mrs. Berger was not the type to say "I told you so" and let it go at that. As soon as they were safely back in their apartment, she repeated every argument she had ever brought up against the tutor.

"I've never been so embarrassed in my life," she declared.

In a matter like this, Mr. Berger knew he could give his wife no quarter.

"*You* were embarrassed," he said. "What about the way you made me feel? All the way home, every time that man said anything to you, you just stuck your nose in the air. Do you think he doesn't notice something like that?"

"I wanted him to notice," Mrs. Berger said. "You're so worried about the way you feel and the way your friend upstairs feels. What about the way I feel and the way poor Marsh feels? How is he going to go back and face that Lensman kid when he knows he's going to be laughing at him?"

Marsh was given several cues like that, but he picked up none of them. Instead he turned on the television to catch the late news and went into the kitchen to fix himself a snack.

"Whatever you say," Mr. Berger declared, "it wasn't as bad as you make it out to be."

"It was *worse*," Mrs. Berger declared roundly. "Once he got started talking, there was no shutting him up. Memory systems and concentration exercises and chronwhatchamacallit."

"Chronology," her husband said.

"And what is that?"

"It's a system of memorizing things in chronological order."

"Big system. He was talking like some kind of a drunk. Except I'd rather be out with a drunk than out with a nut. At least a drunk is sober sometimes."

Marsh turned the volume up on the television set. He was not really watching the program, though. The sound was a barrier between his parents' argument and his own thoughts. With her next remark, however, his mother jumped over the barrier.

"Anyway, one thing is settled," she said. "No more lessons with Mr. Ellman."

"How is that settled?" Mr. Berger asked.

"It's settled because I say it's settled," Mrs. Berger said.

Round and round the argument went and when Mr. Berger joined him in front of the television, Marsh had the impression that his father was only taking a breather between rounds.

"You heard your mother?" Mr. Berger said.

Marsh nodded.

"She doesn't think you should go with Ellman anymore. What do you think?"

"I don't know," Marsh said. "Maybe not."

Mr. Berger sat down heavily on the couch.

"I'll tell you the way I see it," he said. "It's only a couple of weeks to the exam. Ellman's helped you in the past. I know he's kind of a strange duck, but why not make what use you can out of him?"

Marsh pursed his lips. "It's not just for the exam," he said slowly.

His father waited for him to go on.

"The way he was talking tonight," Marsh continued, "he seems to think he's coaching me for the quiz."

In the end it was left up to Marsh, which meant, as Mrs. Berger expressed it, that "as usual, everything is still up in the air."

At one o'clock in the morning, Ellman was still occupied at the table in the center of his living room. On one side of the table was stacked a pile of books dealing with memory systems and on the other side were several texts devoted to rapid reading. Opposite him there was a collection of miscellaneous self-help books which he consulted from time to time. Directly in front of him was a sheaf of notepaper.

By rights, he should have left the gathering as soon as the idea struck him in order to work it out for himself. As it was, he had been compelled to stand there, listening to parental chitchat and forcing himself, every now and then, to toss off one of the intelligent-sounding remarks he had been meditating on earlier in the evening.

"I'm not used to give-and-take," he said. "I'm used to being understood the first time I open my mouth. It's a weakness you fall into when your chief confidant is yourself."

He smiled at the joke and closed the book he had been working with.

"Enough for one night," he said. "I have the program in general outline. All I have to work out now are the specifics. Plenty of time for that."

The new program, he decided, could not be undertaken before the school test. Until then Marsh would have too much pressure on him.

On Monday night the final makeup of the quiz team was announced. Marsh was among the chosen four. The others were Foster Gilson, Dennis Kite and Jerry Tynan. Danny Lensman was the first of the four substitutes.

Marsh tried not to sound sloppy when he told Danny that he should have been picked for the team instead of Marsh.

"Sure I should," Danny said. "But that's their mistake, not mine. Anyway, you'll make out all right. You have your own private coach to help you."

"He helps me just for the S.A.T.," Marsh said.

"Oh, sure," Danny said mockingly. "I forgot."

"I don't need him for this," Marsh said. "There's no way you can train for a quiz anyway."

"Right," Danny said. He was agreeing with Marsh, but the way he agreed was infuriating.

"I *don't* need him," Marsh said. "In fact, I'm getting rid of him in a little while now."

Mrs. Berger, of course, was delighted that Marsh had been chosen, although she admitted that she "wasn't surprised for a minute." Then she rushed off to the telephone to tell everyone that it was official—Marsh would be on television.

While his mother was telephoning, Marsh stretched out on his bed. With the history text propped in front of him, he began to copy extracts from it into a notebook. He made lists of inventors and their inventions, of significant dates and of the functions of the different branches of government.

In the next few days, instead of spending his time on the subway maundering over what had gone on in class that day, he took out his notes and started studying in the only way he had any real confidence in—by rote and repetition.

The signs by which Marsh's withdrawal revealed itself to Ellman were negative at first—the lifelessness in Marsh's recital of class events, the lack of enthusiasm for any new idea Ellman suggested and, eventually, a skipped lesson for which Marsh offered only a flimsy excuse. The tutor, assuming that the boy had entered a "slump," was confident that this difficult time would soon be followed by a second-wind period of exhilaration and progress. But the second wind did not come and, as the days went by, Marsh made small effort to conceal his boredom and impatience.

One night, while Ellman was questioning him about that day's history class, Marsh's answers were particularly curt and testy. The tutor suggested that the boy open the window and take a few deep breaths to clear his head.

Marsh said that his head did not need clearing.

"Then what do you suggest we do?" Ellman asked.

"I suggest we go to bed and forget the whole thing," Marsh said. "I'm tired."

There was arrogance in this, but Ellman recognized it as an arrogance born of strain.

"Of course you're tired," he said. "You've been working very hard. We both have. But we can't waste any time now. It's too close to the test. Only a week."

"The test!" Marsh said, in a nervous, excited voice. "Do you think any of this is going to help with the test?"

"Of course," said Ellman. "What else is it for?"

"I don't know," said Marsh. "Suppose you tell me."

Noticing the look of anguish on the boy's face, Ellman knew that any attempt to continue the lesson would be futile.

"That's all for tonight," he said. "I think you had better go downstairs."

"That's all?" Marsh repeated. "What do you mean, that's all? We just began. Don't you want me to stand on my head on the table and recite all I can remember of the Gettysburg Address? Or maybe I could tell you all the provisions of the Bill of Rights. I know them, you know. I didn't learn them from you, but I know them."

"Marshall, please—" began Ellman.

"Marshall, please," echoed the boy. "Please, Marshall."

Marsh was silent for a moment. When he spoke again it was in his normal tone of voice.

"I don't want to go on with this," he said. "I can study on my own now."

"But, Marshall, it would be so wrong to stop now. You're

only on the brink of realizing how valuable all this has been for you. Sleep now. When you're rested and feel better, we'll talk about it and you'll see what progress we've made."

"Progress!" Marsh answered. "I made more progress in three weeks on my own than I've made in five weeks with you."

At that moment Ellman ceased to notice Marsh's physical symptoms. He paid no attention to the boy's tone of voice and listened only for the words as Marsh told him how for the past week and a half all his advice had been ignored and his projects set aside. Several times Ellman tried to interrupt, but Marsh's flow of words could not be stopped. At each attempt Ellman raised his voice to a higher pitch. When he finally broke through, he was nearly shouting.

"Do you *realize?*" he said. "Do you realize what you've been doing? You've been making a fool of me! Wasting my time! Cheating and lying and putting us both through this ridiculous farce!"

"Wasting time!" Marsh shouted. "*You* talk about wasting time! I came to you to learn two subjects and what did I ever learn about them? What did you ever teach me?"

"I was trying to teach you something more important than any particular *subject*. Something that would help you with *all* your subjects. I was doing what any good teacher does. I was teaching you to *use your own mind.*"

Marsh flicked this off with such an expressive gesture of impatience that Ellman could not restrain himself.

"Of course," he added, "I was working under the possibly erroneous assumption that you *had* a mind."

As soon as he had spoken the words, Ellman realized their injustice. He tried to retract them, but the boy did not give him time.

"Let it go," Marsh said.

Ellman could not move quickly enough to stop Marsh from

leaving. He stood at the railing calling after him as the boy ran down the stairs, but Marsh did not stop.

"Good!" Callahan said when Ellman told him about Marsh's departure of the previous evening. "You're well out of it. Now stay out of it."

Ellman did not want to stay out of it. He protested to Callahan, even to the point of himself assuming responsibility for Marsh's actions. "I failed him," he declared. "It was not enough for me to be satisfied that he was making progress. It was part of my duty to make that clear to *him*."

Callahan made the mistake of affirming that it was really nobody's fault. "There was just too much pressure on him, between the exam and the quiz program."

"Exactly," said Ellman. "I should have understood that. Marshall understood it, of course, but he could hardly be expected to cope with it. Marshall feels I failed him where the examination is concerned. He'll know better when he takes the test. In my own sense, I succeeded. I was in the act of succeeding."

"There is no success except the success Marshall asked for," Callahan said. "Accept that. And accept the fact that it's all finished with."

"Marshall will come back," Ellman insisted. "You don't understand these things. I have a plan to teach him memory and speed reading. When I spoke to his father about the memory course he was very interested. Besides, Marshall knows—maybe unconsciously, but he *knows*—the way my concentration exercises have helped him. That alone will be enough to bring him back. Take my word for it. Tomorrow night he'll be there. A little sheepish, maybe, but nevertheless willing to pretend that nothing has happened so long as I play the game along with him."

"Ellman, listen to yourself, will you? 'Marshall knows I

failed. He'll be back because I succeeded. The memory course he hasn't even started yet will bring him back.' You're feeding yourself on empty hopes."

"Empty hopes?" Ellman said. "Listen, you've never been to my house. Come tomorrow night. You'll see. Marshall will come up at the regular time for his lesson. Meet him then. You can judge for yourself if it's empty hopes or not."

Callahan arrived at seven-thirty the next evening. He surveyed Ellman's apartment with awe and envy. "The *room* you have here!" he said. "The size of that kitchen! Even the bathroom here is bigger than my whole place!"

More than anything else he was attracted to the table in the living room.

"We used to always have a big table in the living room when I was a kid," he said. "Now nobody has them."

He even lifted the tablecloth to peek under it. "It has a *pad* under it!" he exclaimed. "Jeez, I forgot all about that. When I was a kid, that's where we used to put all the letters and papers and things like that. You'd hear my father yelling, 'Where's the gas bill?' and my mother would answer, 'Under the pad on the living room table.' Any time anthing was missing, it was, 'Did you look under the pad on the living room table?' Many's the time we'd knock the lamp over trying to lift the pad and my father would yell at us for being too damned lazy to move it out of the way."

Ellman found Callahan's heartiness uncomfortable, even though he was touched by his friend's apparent desire to bind the two of them together with a common heritage of padded tables. Was it to be a case of the older generation closing ranks against the younger?

"I usually take the pad off before Marshall comes up." Ellman said. He proceeded to do so.

Callahan started fiddling with the tape recorder.

"Is this one of the tapes you were telling me about?" he asked. "How do you turn it on?"

Ellman demonstrated the operation of the recorder.

"Play one of the tapes, why don't you?" Callahan asked.

Ellman tried to sound firm. "Marshall is coming up any minute," he said.

"Until he comes," Callahan urged.

Ellman shrugged. "Until he comes," he said.

Under the spell of the music, Ellman forgot Callahan's presence completely. He thought again of the quarrel with Marsh and he daydreamed long conversations that he wished he might have with Marsh and Mr. Berger. He humbled himself, confessed his limited education and discoursed on his thwarted ambition. Then, with the new strength of honesty to support him, he persuaded them of the wonderful things he could do for Marsh if only he had another chance. He was logical and eloquent as he explained the reasons for their past difficulties—pressure, urgency, anxiety—but even as he dreamed the words he knew that these conversations would never take place.

Callahan looked at his watch. It was nine-thirty. He looked at Ellman.

"You didn't really think he'd come, did you?" he asked.

"I thought he wanted a teacher," Ellman said. "I saw myself as a molder and shaper of minds. An influence, a Socrates. I thought if I could open his mind—"

"Ellman, it's no tragedy. Even without the quarrel it was about to end now. Soon the kid will take the test. That would have been the end of it right there."

"That was the deadline," Ellman agreed. "If I didn't get to him by then, I never would. But, my friend, I did get to him. This urgency—"

"Urgency?"

"Mine, not Marshall's. I feel such great urgency to *use* it all."

"Use what?"

"If it all fades with me, then it all means nothing."

Ellman turned the tape off. "A few private tapes, that's all there is left of Jacob," he said. "He left no real heritage. His sons prove that. They could be anybody's sons."

Callahan was not alarmed by the disjointed nature of Ellman's comments. He knew that he was hearing only a part of what was racing through the old man's mind, that in a way Ellman was merely repeating headlines from his thinking.

"Come give me another cup of coffee," he said. "Then I have to be on my way. Tell me, how is it in this neighborhood? Do you think I'll get to the subway all in one piece?"

"I'm old-fashioned enough to want to expand the mind with knowledge and ideas," Ellman said, "not with drugs."

Slowly Callahan got his friend into the kitchen and involved him in the business of making coffee. By the time they sat down at the kitchen table to drink the coffee, Ellman was giving his friend a sad "you think you know me" look.

"I've been foolish," Ellman said. "I remind myself of an old man I read about in a newspaper once. He was arrested for committing a lewd act in a public place."

Callahan smiled.

"Oh, I thought a great deal about that man and his foolishness," Ellman continued slowly. "In those days I kept a diary and I remember writing in it something to the effect that there *ought* to be a time in one's life when one is free of all inhibitions. If we can't have a saturnalia every year, let's at least have a certain time in each life when all foolishness is easily forgotten and forgiven."

If Ellman's tone of voice had been different, Callahan would have taken this as the theme for a discussion. But Ellman's tone was one of public meditation, and Callahan let him go on without interruption.

"Perhaps because I was young then myself, I thought the

time of freedom should be in one's youth. Now I think it should be in age. Young people today have all the freedom they need, and the result is that no one dares even to guess what tomorrow will bring. Looking at them, I see that when I thought of a time of freedom, I assumed that later there would be a return to the restraints of society. I never saw it tearing society apart altogether."

"Well, society was a stronger thing in our day."

"And I think, unconsciously, I must have been counting on guilt to set in and do its work. The puritanical conscience assuming that everybody else has a puritanical conscience."

"You think Marshall has that kind of conscience?" Callahan asked.

"Marshall has nothing to do with it," Ellman said. "If he comes back at all, he'll come back on my terms."

Part Two

Chapter 12

Even though the weather was still cold, Mr. Berger felt a warm glow as he returned home that evening. The rumor that the Playton Box Company was going to move out of town had turned out to be only a rumor after all. Mr. Daigle, the tall, humorless president of the company, had called all the employees together that afternoon to tell them, man to man, that their jobs were secure.

"We will not now, or at any time in the foreseeable future, contemplate any move out of the city," he said. To emphasize the point, he announced that their lease on the present premises had at least another eighteen months to go and that, furthermore, all the officers of the company were New York residents.

"The union must have got to them," Gene Quinn told Mr. Berger after the meeting.

"Well, we're good for another eighteen months, anyway," Mr. Berger said.

He was therefore in the best of spirits as he rounded the corner on the way to his house. Everything seemed to be going all right.

He was surprised to find Ellman waiting for him in the street in front of their house. The old man looked tired and drawn.

"Kinda chilly to be hanging around in the street, isn't it?" Mr. Berger asked as he approached him.

"I wanted to talk to you," Ellman said.

"Something about the lessons?" Mr. Berger asked. "How are they going, anyway?"

Ellman looked surprised. "Marshall didn't tell you?" he asked.

"Tell me what?"

Ellman hesitated. "Marshall and I had a little . . . misunderstanding the other night. I think that the strain was a little too much for him."

Mr. Berger was puzzled. "What strain?" he asked.

"Too much studying, too much tension over the examination, and now this quiz program . . . He said he didn't want to go on with the lessons."

Mr. Berger turned abruptly. "When was all this?"

"Monday night," Ellman said.

"What about last night?"

"He didn't come up last night. Mr. Berger, I have a rather strange proposition to make to you and believe me, it's not myself I'm thinking of, it's Marshall."

Mr. Berger said nothing.

"Let him forget the lessons for a while," Ellman continued. "He can take the examination and get that off his mind. Between you and me, I'm sure he's qualified now to be accepted at any college in the country."

Mr. Berger beamed modestly. "Well, I'm glad you feel that way about it," he said, smiling.

"But then, after the examination is over, let him come back to me for more lessons."

"What for?" Mr. Berger asked. "Just to raise his final grades, you mean?"

"To raise his final grades, to help him with the quiz program and to prepare him for college. Today, when you go to college, you need more than knowledge, Mr. Berger. You need skills. Reading skills and memory skills."

"I saw one of those rapid reading things on television once. This guy was just running his finger down each page and as fast as he could turn the pages he was reading the book."

"I can teach Marshall to read like that. As fast as that. And to remember what he reads."

Mr. Berger was carrying a newspaper under his arm. With a sudden aggressive motion, Ellman snatched the paper from him. For a moment Mr. Berger thought he was to be given an on-the-spot demonstration of Ellman's reading abilities. Instead Ellman handed the paper back to him.

"Open to page two," he said.

Mr. Berger obeyed unquestioningly.

"Is there an advertisement there?"

"No."

"What's the biggest story about?"

"The war in the Middle East."

Ellman took a second to register this. "Good," he said. "Is there an advertisement on page three?"

Page three described a murder in Queens, page four carried a Washington column and page five had an advertisement for a camera store. There were forty-eight pages to the paper and Ellman insisted that Mr. Berger name him one item from each page. Berger, who was quick to see which way Ellman was leading, cooperated without protest.

"Now," Ellman said, when they had finished. "Name me a page."

"Twenty-seven," Mr. Berger said.

"Movie advertisements."

"Sixteen?"

"A bank is giving away percolators."

"Forty-four?"

"An account of a prizefight."

"Twenty-four?"

"Editorials and letters to the editor."

When Mr. Berger finished calling numbers out at random, Ellman took him through the paper once more, from beginning to end, repeating the items that Mr. Berger had supplied him with earlier.

"Pretty good," Mr. Berger said when Ellman finished. "It's some kind of a trick, isn't it?"

"Of course it's a trick," Ellman said. "But it's a trick that works. Those forty-eight items from the newspaper could have been forty-eight events from history. They could have been chemical elements or great books or anything you like. I can teach Marshall that trick. That and a great many others like it."

"Never mind Marsh. I'd like to learn that one myself."

Ellman smiled, a wide, disarming smile. "Perhaps someday," he said. "But right now it's Marshall we have to think about."

Mr. Berger frowned. "I'll talk to him," he said. "Personally, I think he'd be a damned fool to pass up a chance like this, but anyhow the decision has to be his."

Ellman shrugged in his best benevolent-old-man style.

"Don't press him for a decision," he said. "We want to ease the tension, not add to it."

"I don't see why he shouldn't go for it," Mr. Berger said. "In fact, I'm almost sure he will. I can almost promise you."

Chilly as it was, Ellman lingered in the street for a long while after Mr. Berger had passed into the building and gone up to his apartment. It was dark and quiet now and Ellman enjoyed the cold wind that was blowing through the street. Never had his brain felt so cool and clear. In the quiet of the street he could hear his own voice shouting out the key words he had spent the entire day rehearsing—the number code from the book *Instant Memory*.

"So I'm reduced to doing tricks," he said. "So what? If they prefer tricks to real teaching, then I'll teach them tricks. But I'll still be a real teacher."

It was Mrs. Berger's bingo night. Mr. Berger waited until after she had left, then joined Marsh in the living room.

"It's bad for your eyes to sit so close to the TV set," he said. "Those color sets give off radiation too."

Marsh moved back a bit but said nothing.

"I told you about that rumor that the company might move out of town, didn't I?" Mr. Berger said.

"Yeah. You told me," Marsh said.

"Turned out to be just a rumor after all."

"Good."

"They had a meeting today to kill the rumor. After the meeting one of the messengers came over to me. A real punk of a guy. I think I told you about him—his name is Lanny. Well, he comes over to me and says, 'Good thing for you the company is staying put. At your age you'd never get another job.'"

Marsh shook his head in a way that said nothing more than that he was aware that his father had spoken.

"Funny thing, here I was thinking the same thing about him. Punk kids with no real education and no experience, what kind of a chance have they got? And they think *I'm* the one who wouldn't be able to get a job. They don't know the first thing about it."

Marsh was aware that his father was trying to elicit some response, but he was not sure what the desired reaction was. If he expressed confidence in his father's ability to find a new job, it might seem that he was taking too much for granted, that he did not understand the difficulties involved. On the other hand, his father's pride might be considerably damaged on hearing his own son express doubt as to his ability to support his family.

"It's rough," Marsh said.

"Damn rough," his father agreed. "Oh, I'd find a job one way or another, don't worry about that. But it probably wouldn't be as good as this one. I wouldn't have the seniority I have in this one. Or the security."

Marsh grinned. "How can it be secure?" he asked. "They don't give a pension and for all you know they were ready to move out of town without a minute's notice."

"We got a union," Mr. Berger said. "The union has a pension fund. And it's the union that prevents them from moving out of town. But that's not what I meant. Maybe I shouldn't have said security. Some other word." Mr. Berger thought hard, but all he came up with was a question. "What do you call it when you work for a company for a long time and you build up something? Not security . . ."

"Equity?" Marsh suggested.

"That's it!" Mr. Berger said. "You build up equity. That's what I got with this company."

That satisfied Mr. Berger, who lapsed into a silence, but it left Marsh puzzled. Unless it was a synonym for "security," Marsh had no idea what the word "equity" meant. Nor did he have any idea where he had come across the phrase "building up equity." The word had just popped into his head.

That sort of thing had been happening to him quite often lately, especially at quiz practice.

"I met your friend Ellman when I was coming home from work tonight," Mr. Berger said. "He told me you haven't been up there for a while."

Marsh turned from the television set and gave his father his full attention.

"I was going to tell you about it," he said. "I just didn't know how."

"Look, Marsh, nobody's forcing you to study with Ellman. If you don't want to, you don't have to. You don't have to find any special way to explain it to me. Just say, 'I'm finished with Ellman.' That's all there is to it."

Marsh smiled, but he did not repeat the formula.

"What did he say tonight?"

"Just that you had some sort of argument, that's all."

"It's nothing on Ellman," Marsh said. "It's just that it was getting to be too much, that's all."

"That's what he said. Almost his very words. Too much pressure, too much tension. That's why he thinks it might be better if you didn't go back at all now until after you get the college thing out of the way."

"Go back?" Marsh repeated. "What for?"

Marsh leaned forward and turned down the volume of the television set.

Mr. Berger rose from his chair. "Marsh," he said. "You've got a big opportunity working with Ellman and you'd be a fool to pass it up."

"What opportunity?" Marsh asked.

"That man can teach you things you never dreamed of."

"What things?"

"How would you like to be able to memorize a whole newspaper after reading it only once?"

Marsh's expression implied that such trickery was beneath discussion even if it was interesting.

"He did it for me," Mr. Berger continued. "Right in front of my own eyes. And that's not all. He can teach you to speed read. How would you like to be able to read a whole book in one hour? A whole book!"

Marsh could not dismiss the value of such abilities. He admitted that he had been intrigued by people with trained memories, but he pointed out to his father that courses in memory training and speed reading were available to the public any time they wanted to take them.

"Do you know what they cost?" his father asked. "Here you get it for nothing, with a private teacher and everything."

"But how do you know Ellman can *teach* these things? Even if he can do it himself, that doesn't mean he can teach it."

"He learned. He knows how he learned. You can learn the same way he did."

The best Mr. Berger could get from Marsh by way of commitment was an admission that he was interested and that he would consider it.

In the next few days, Marsh could not put the idea of memory training and rapid reading out of his mind. Every time he saw someone on the subway plodding through a book, he daydreamed of himself flicking rapidly through the pages and then announcing, a scant minute or so after he had started reading it, "It was good. I enjoyed it very much."

He saw himself with a photographic memory, reading six books a day and memorizing every book he read. "Oh, yes," he would say when Mr. Reedy challenged his answers during quiz practice. "It's not a common practice, but it *is* a valid one. You'll find it described in the second-year chemistry textbook. Page two hundred and forty-three, second paragraph down."

In these daydreams, all the sweat and strain was behind him and he always spoke with the voice of quiet authority, expressing a secure calm available only to those who are absolutely sure of their facts. "No, the line isn't from Whitman, it's from Poe. 'The Raven.' You'll find it in the poetry section of *Learning Through Literature*, page five hundred and sixty-two."

Marsh could not escape the daydreams, but neither could he escape the obstacle that stood in the way of their coming true —Ellman. Could Ellman really unlock those doors for him? Inevitably Marsh found himself asking the question "If he can really do these things, why doesn't he use that power the way I would? How come he lives the way he does?"

The answer was a shrug. Ellman was Ellman, a strange old man. Maybe his mother was right, after all, and Marsh might become like Ellman himself. It was not a risk he would rush blindly into.

One afternoon after quiz practice he went up to Mr. Reedy and asked if he might speak to him for a moment.

"Do you think it's worthwhile to learn how to read fast?" he asked the teacher. "I mean you see all those advertisements about how you can double and triple your reading speed. Is there really anything to that?"

"Yes, of course there is."

"What about these memory courses you read about?"

"Now wait a minute," Mr. Reedy said. "One thing at a time. First let me ask you: is this a theoretical question or are you thinking of taking a reading course?"

"Yes. I'm thinking of taking . . . lessons."

"Okay." Mr. Reedy's voice had the authoritative tone of someone blocking out a program. "Now, personally, I don't know what your schedule is, but you're in your last year of high school now." Mr. Reedy stopped. Some bit of information was missing from his program. "You're planning to go to college, of course?"

"Yes."

"Have you been accepted at any college yet?"

"I expect to go to City College."

Mr. Reedy frowned. "You're not putting all your eggs in one basket, I hope. You've talked to the adviser, have you, about state loans, grants, scholarships and things like that?"

"Yeah, only—" Marsh did not want to think about the possibility of not being accepted at City. "About the reading course," he said.

Mr. Reedy turned his computer on again and went back to summarizing Marsh's situation.

"You've not been accepted at any college yet," he said.

"You've got your final examinations to study for and, of course, there's 'Scholarship Quiz' coming up. Personally, I can't imagine where you'd even find *time* for a reading course."

"But suppose it only took like one or two nights a week?"

"The class would meet one or two nights a week, you mean," Mr. Reedy said. "Between those nights you'd be expected to spend a lot of time practicing. All in all, I think the best thing would be to put the course off until the summertime."

Mr. Reedy cocked his head over on the side. Marsh, fearing that the next question would be "Where are you planning to take this course?" headed him off.

"What about a memory course?" Marsh asked.

Mr. Reedy looked pained. "To put it frankly," he said, "my own opinion is that most of these memory courses you hear about are just plain junk. They're not worth the time you'll spend on them and they're certainly not worth the money."

"But a reading course would be worthwhile?"

"It's not as simple as that," Mr. Reedy hedged. "A lot depends on who's teaching the course and what method they use. There are some good, reliable schools and then again there are some fly-by-night operations that'll do you more harm than good. And either way it's likely to be an expensive proposition."

"But if it's somebody who really knows—"

"Who?" Mr. Reedy asked.

Marsh tried to act as though he had not heard the question.

"What school are you planning to go to?" Mr. Reedy asked.

"I wasn't thinking of going to any particular school," Marsh said. "It was just the idea of taking the course."

"Okay," Mr. Reedy said. "But I wouldn't recommend starting before the end of the school year. If you're still interested in the idea then, you can come to me and I'll be happy to supply you with the names of a few worthwhile schools."

Marsh had no option for selectivity. As long as the course was a worthwhile one, he decided to take it with Ellman. That night he told his father, "Tell Ellman it's okay. I can start the Monday after next."

Chapter 13

The first thing Ellman decided he would have to do was to give Marsh a book and watch him read it. If there were no perceptible lip movements, then it would be foolish even to mention them to Marsh. This discipline was so obvious that it was covered in all the books Ellman had on the subject. Ellman pulled them all from the shelf, stacked them on the table and began flipping through the pages of each.

"If I could practice what I teach," he said aloud, "I'd be able to read and memorize them all with no trouble."

At one time an uncle had recommended reading aloud to Ellman as a possible cure for stuttering, and he had never got over the habit of "hearing" what he read. Once, many years ago, he had heard Lionel Barrymore reading Dickens' *Christmas Carol* on the radio. Soon after that, he borrowed a copy of the book from the library and read it, all the while hearing in his mind the voice of Lionel Barrymore speaking the words. Then, for a while, he cast an actor in the role of "reader" for almost every book he read, a habit that greatly increased his enjoyment of books.

He had Paul Muni to read him Dostoevsky, Walter Huston to read him Sinclair Lewis, and Ronald Colman to read him poetry. C. Aubrey Smith read Kipling to him, and Joseph Conrad was never so enjoyable as when Charles Laughton played the narrator's part in his stories. Every novel of social significance had John Garfield's touch to it, and all humorous material was somehow funnier if he could get Frank Morgan to read it for him.

There were antic specialties too, like James Stewart's awkward version of Emerson, Wallace Beery's unexpectedly successful reading of *Huckleberry Finn,* and the time when Ellman had become bored with *Silas Marner* and was about to leave it unfinished when W. C. Fields stepped up to the podium and rendered the second half of that pathetic novel hilarious.

That was long ago, however, and for a time Ellman forgot about it completely. Then it all came back to him during the McCarthy era, when he could not rid himself of the vague fear that Edward G. Robinson might be called up before the House Un-American Activities Committee to account for certain readings he had given of the works of Karl Marx. Ellman knew these readings had taken place nowhere but in his own mind, yet so strong was the power of his imagination that he could remember them as vividly as if he had heard them at a public performance.

If this practice had increased Ellman's enjoyment of reading and made unforgettable memories of many of the books he had read, it was nevertheless fatal to any possibility of increasing his reading speed. At any rate, there had come a time when the process seemed too arduous. It was often harder for Ellman to select a reader than to select a book. Sometimes he would begin a book with one reader in mind and then switch two or three times before coming to the end. Once he had found himself in the library wishing he could think of a way to explain to the librarian that he wanted to borrow a book that would sound good read in the voice of Franchot Tone.

Confronted now with eight texts on the subject of rapid reading, Ellman contented himself with reading the tables of contents, the chapter headings and a sentence or two here and there. It would have suited him better to be able to read only the first sentence of each paragraph, but these were the kind of easy-to-read books in which few paragraphs were more than one sentence long.

He whipped through the first book easily enough, and the second. But by the time he got to the third, his conscience was troubling him.

"The man took the trouble to write down each word," he said. "The least I can do is read them all."

He did not like to *use* a book, to treat it like a thing. A book was a person talking to him and it deserved to be treated with respect.

Ellman left the books and meditated for a while over his coffee.

Some books were meant to be used, to be squeezed for all you could get out of them and then discarded. It was not conversation and companionship that Marsh wanted from books, it was information. As a speed reader, he would not use his skill on novels and poetry but on textbooks.

In Ellman's youth a textbook was something that was handed out at the beginning of the term accompanied by a lecture about how the books were school property and students were not expected to mark, soil or damage them in any way. Even in his first acquaintance with them, therefore, Ellman had seen books as sacred objects. He had once thought this a fine attitude. But he saw now that it could be carried too far.

That was the first thing he had to teach Marsh—to approach books with audacity.

Ellman went once more to the bookshelf and stood in front of it for a long time. Eventually he took down an old paperback mystery that had been passed around at the post office years ago and eventually found its way into Ellman's hands. He had read it and then found that he had no one to pass it on to. Since books were not the kind of things he could bring himself to throw away, it had come to rest on his bookshelf.

He held the book in his hands and stared at the cover. It was a garish picture of a voluptuous seminude that had nothing whatever to do with the book's quaint old English murder-in-the-village plot.

Ellman opened the book to the center, held both sides carefully in his hands and told himself he was going to tear it up.

"A respect for books is like a respect for any *object*," he said. "It prevents development."

The muscles of his arm stiffened. He was ready to pull the two pieces apart. And yet he hesitated. Something more than respect was stopping him. There was also the sense of waste. It was as though a voice were saying to him, "Someone could enjoy that book. It's a shame to waste it. Waste like that is a sin."

Ellman sat down again with the book before him.

"It cost me nothing," he said. "It was given to me free. And if I tried to sell it, I wouldn't get two cents for it. It's the kind of book dealers buy by weight, so much to the pound. So where is the great waste if I just tear it up and throw it away now? Whose loss is it?"

The answer lay in his hands, in the open pages before him. The book was still readable, still capable of giving pleasure—"to anyone who doesn't know who the murderer is." And that fact alone made it worth preserving.

"There are hospitals and homes that are always looking for books to pass out."

The title of one of the other books on the table caught his eyes and brought him back to the main project in hand: *Sight Lines, The Key to Flash Reading.*

"Sentimental foolishness," Ellman said. With a spasmodic jerk, he pulled apart *The Dowling Murders.*

The movement sent a shock through his spine that Ellman

had not anticipated. The aftermath of the shock brought a smile to his face. Quickly he began stripping out pages and ripping each page in two.

"There," he said, when he had finished the work of destruction. "I've done it. Or maybe I should say, 'That's torn it.'"

How surprised Marsh would be when he learned that at his first reading lesson, all he would be required to do would be to tear up books. Ellman went to the bookshelf and began to select the books to be destroyed.

"We kill two birds with one stone," he said. "Marshall gets a valuable lesson and I get more space on my bookshelves."

Very rapidly he selected fifteen books for Marsh to tear up. Before he went to sleep, he removed them from the shelf and piled them neatly on the floor in front of the piano.

While he was waiting for the test papers to be handed out, Marsh recalled a newsreel he had seen on television only a few days ago. A line of pickets was marching in front of the main gate at City College carrying signs that read LOWER THE BARRIERS, OPEN ADMISSIONS and FREE EDUCATION FOR ALL. The commentator said that most of the pickets were actually students at the college. But, to show that there was not unanimity on the issue, the camera focused on another group of students who were heckling the pickets.

"It's not the barriers you want lowered," one of the hecklers called. "It's the standards."

Even now, facing the test that would ultimately determine whether or not he was eligible for City College, Marsh had to agree with the hecklers.

It was stupid, he thought. If these people wanted to help others to get a better education, it would be more to the point to organize study groups instead of picket lines.

Suddenly, it was as though he had been explaining and describing all this to Ellman. The image of the old man appeared in Marsh's eyes and he could hear his voice speaking.

"The one doesn't necessarily preclude the other. Maybe they've organized study groups *as well as* picket lines."

"Well, *one* of them is just a waste of time."

A student aide put a copy of the test face down on Marsh's desk. As he looked up, Marsh saw that the aide was grinning at him. Marsh flushed, realizing that he had spoken his last thought aloud.

He had expected the test to be concerned solely with information about the subjects he had studied in school. Instead, the first three sections had all the earmarks of an "intelligence test," which meant that the simplest-looking questions were likely to turn out to be the trickiest. What is most like this or most unlike that? What is the next number in this series? There was the usual proportion of unfair questions for which there seemed to be more than one correct answer and Marsh sweated and suffered over them, trying with all his might to think like a teacher, so that he could understand what shade of meaning was intended in the question. But it was all in vain, of course. Marsh had worried his way through tests like this before. In the end you simply put the pencil mark in the best place you could think of and some weeks later you learned what you scored on the test. There was never any way of finding which questions you got right and which you got wrong.

The information section was much easier, except for the subjects Marsh had never studied, like French, and the ones he had long since forgotten, like ancient history. Had it been a final examination at his own school, Marsh would have left the test room confident that he had passed. Whether he had scored high enough to raise his average to the City College level, however, was another matter entirely.

In the morning, Ellman looked through the fifteen books he had selected for Marsh, and put five of them back on the shelf.

"Marshall wouldn't see it as a part of the lesson at all," he said. "He'd think it was a household job I want him to do for me before we get down to the lessons."

Before the day was over, Ellman had put four more books back on the shelf.

"What I'll have him do is tear one book up at the beginning of each lesson. Like a little ceremony to mark the opening of each class."

In the end, he put the remaining books back also. They could always be taken down again as they were needed, one at a time.

"Well, did you pass the test?" Marsh's mother asked.

"I don't know," Marsh answered.

"What do you mean you don't know? Was it easy or hard?"

"There were some questions on subjects I never took, like French, but most of them I could answer. I didn't do too bad."

"Then you passed."

"It's not a matter of passing or failing," Marsh explained. "It's just how high a score you get."

"But how do you know whether you're getting into City College or not?"

"The tests go to Albany to be graded. When the grades come back, the school sends them to City College along with your transcript. Then City College lets you know whether you're in or not."

"And how long does it all take?"

"All these questions," Marsh said, waving his arms in the air.

"I got a right to ask questions," his mother said. "How long?"

"It usually takes a couple of weeks."

"But they notify you either way?"

Marsh didn't know the answer to that one.

"In two or three weeks, if you're accepted they notify you."

"And if you're not?"

"If they notify you, you're accepted. If not, forget it."

"That's not right. They ought to notify you either way."

Marsh had wanted to sound strong and confident and not dwell on the possibility of failure, but he realized now that he had made a mistake in giving his mother the impression that the college would write him only if he was accepted. He had a vision of his mother opening the mailbox, finding a letter from the college addressed to Marsh and running around to tell all the neighbors he had been accepted at City College, only to have Marsh himself come home, open the envelope and read a rejection notice.

"I don't know," he said. "Maybe they notify you both ways. In fact, now I think about it I'm *sure* they do."

The books on the three-for-a-quarter rack were the most meaningless books Ellman had ever thumbed through—empty westerns and garishly covered "hard-boiled" mysteries. Some of them had been stained with a dark-blue dye and still others had had their covers torn off. And though he looked through the whole of two large racks, Ellman did not find a single title or author that was in any way familiar to him at all.

"Such books would be a waste of money at any price," Ellman said to himself.

He left the store and began walking back up the street toward the subway. Even if he had to pay a little more for Marsh's books, it would be worth it. There was nothing at all to be learned from destroying books like these. Ellman felt that even he himself could have torn them up without the least qualm. It was an interesting theory, but he would not spend a quarter to prove it. Just in case he was wrong, he did not want to be left with three unexplainably awful books on his shelf.

Marsh would have torn them for him, of course. Ellman could imagine him ripping into them without the least hesitation.

And then suddenly, Ellman could imagine Marsh ripping into his own books too without the least hesitation. It was quite possible that Ellman's precious collection would be as empty and meaningless to Marsh as the books he had just been looking at were to Ellman. It was even possible that Marsh might have found that faceless assembly of westerns and mysteries more interesting and attractive than Ellman's own books.

Marsh was taking Donna to a movie that night. Because she had an after-school job, they met in front of the theater. It was eight o'clock.

"I nearly got fired today," Donna said. "This *woman* came up to the counter and she said she wanted a package of pinch curlers. So I told her I didn't think we had any in stock."

"What are pinch curlers?"

"It's an old-fashioned curler they used to use. At first even I didn't know what they were. So anyway, I told her I didn't think we had any. I didn't even think they *made* them anymore. And she got very nasty. 'Who ever heard of a five-and-dime that didn't carry pinch curlers?' she said. So I told her, 'This isn't a five-and-dime, this is a department store.' They don't like you to call it anything else. Besides, they say it sounds better for us to be able to say 'I work in a department store' than 'I work in a five-and-ten.' Big deal. Anyway, she starts screaming and yelling that she wants to see the manager. Meanwhile, people are turning around and starting to look at us. You'd think I was killing the old bitch. So I tried to get her to calm down. I said, 'I'll look behind the counter, maybe you'll be in luck, I'll find something.' Well, at that point, Artie comes over and he says, 'What seems to be the trouble, madam?' I told you about Artie. He's the floor man in our section. 'What seems to be the trouble, madam?' he says. Just the way he said it I wanted to laugh, he looked so serious. 'I wanted to buy some pinch curlers, but this *salesgirl* says you don't have any.' You should have heard the way she said 'salesgirl.' Like I was the Creature from the Black Lagoon or something."

"So what did Artie do?"

"He checked around and then he said he'd go back to check inventory or something. I think he just went to the other end of the store and checked out Gloria for a while. That's his girl."

"What did the woman do?"

"Oh, she just stood by the counter waiting. She didn't have anything to say to *me*. She must have figured Artie was some kind of a big wheel and she was dealing only with the wheels. Finally Artie came back and said we don't keep them in stock anymore."

"And that's what you call nearly getting fired?"

"The best is yet to come," Donna said. "After Artie told her we didn't have them in stock, she had the nerve to look at me and say, 'This young lady could have told me that.' Then she said to Artie, 'Thank you very much. *You've* been very kind.' So I yell after her, 'Next time try an antique shop.'"

Marsh laughed.

"Well, *that* got her," Donna said. "She stopped dead in her tracks, she turned around and she started letting me have it. And I let her have it right back. You know me when I get started."

Marsh knew only too well.

"Then before you know it, she had the manager and everyone else out. So this afternoon I was in the manager's office."

"And they *didn't* fire you?"

"Why should they? I didn't start it, she did. Besides, Artie backed me up. But I'm what they call 'on warning,' so I probably will be fired any time now."

Marsh bought the tickets but as he and Donna entered the movie Donna was still raging.

"Stupid thing! Why can't she use rollers like everybody else? No, she has to have pinch curlers. Why? Because that's what they used to use twenty years ago."

"Serves her right for trying to act her age," Marsh said unhelpfully.

"Age, nothing. Everybody uses rollers nowadays."

"Not everybody."

"What do you know about it anyway? You don't know nothing about nothing."

Marsh laughed. "That's the way I felt when I first looked at that test," he said. "Hey, how come you didn't ask me about that?"

"What test?"

"The S. A. T. I took it today."

"And you passed it?"

"I think so."

"Good. I'm glad. Let's sit in the balcony. I want to smoke."

They went into the movie.

Ellman was sitting on the edge of the bed and laughing uncontrollably.

Prompted by the realization that he was giving too much thought to which books Marsh would destroy and too little thought to which ones he would read, he had begun pacing through his apartment, pronouncing deep thoughts about the quality of a man's thinking being determined by the quality of his reading, when suddenly he had caught sight of himself in the bedroom mirror.

"Reading," he said loudly. "It's made me what I am today." Then he began to laugh. Before long the laugh developed into a roar of ferocious heartiness and energy so vigorous that he had to sit on the edge of the bed lest he lose his balance. It was not the laugh of an old man at all.

"I could be laughing myself right into a heart attack," Ellman said, and then he laughed at his own fear, foolishly glad that he was able to laugh at all.

"It's my younger self coming out," he said. "Look at me, I'm forty years younger." The young Julius Ellman was laughing at the old one, at what reading had made him and what foolishness it had led him into.

The strangeness of laughing by oneself and declaring oneself to be forty years younger—the soft-cover psychologists would say he was giving way to fantasy.

"So what?" he said, laughing some more. "That's what life is for—giving away."

Ellman felt freer and more himself than he had in years and he kept trying to find ways to keep the laughter flowing. But eventually the words and ways became more self-conscious. The laughter died out and left him sitting quietly on the edge of the bed, enjoying the feeling of the warm blood circulating around his smile.

"That was good," he said at length. "But it's not helping Marshall any."

Mr. Berger had never known Marsh's homework to call for so much activity. The boy kept jumping distractedly from one book to another, pausing to cogitate every once in a while and then leaping at a book. Once he came into the living room to ask if either of his parents knew what had happened to the *World Almanac* they used to have. Another time he dashed into his own room to search through his closet and his drawers, emerging after a while with a battered old geometry workbook. Several times Mr. Berger was tempted to say something to him but Marsh, whether he knew it or not, was grinning. Don't spoil the pleasure, Mr. Berger told himself.

While he was in the process of getting himself a beer, however, Mr. Berger saw Marsh go into no fewer than three different textbooks and scribble a note from each.

He could not stand it any longer.

"What kind of homework is this?" he asked.

Marsh stopped working but the smile remained on his face. "It's not regular homework," he said. "It's for the quiz."

Mr. Berger understood even less now than he had before.

"You're trying to study everything at once?" he asked.

"No. I'm making up questions," Marsh answered. "The teacher says every time we come to practice now, we have to bring thirty questions with us."

"Thirty?" It seemed a high figure.

"Ten for the singles round, ten for the doubles and ten for the team round."

"Oh." Thirty was now a reasonable number.

Muttering something about letting Marsh get back to his work while he got back to his television, Mr. Berger returned to the living room. But Mrs. Berger had overheard their conversation.

"What kind of a test is it where they let you make up your own questions?" she demanded.

Carefully Marsh explained that none of the questions he was preparing would be asked of anybody on his own team.

"We make up questions for their team and they make up questions for ours. So you try to make them hard—but not too hard, because that wouldn't be fair."

The next day during quiz practice, Jerry Tynan and Foster Gilson and their two practice teammates answered all of Marsh's questions without hesitation, beating Marsh's team by a considerable margin. Apparently the members of Gilson's team had come together and made a joint effort in concocting their questions, because they were all similar in style. They were not difficult questions, but they were phrased in such a way that one was tempted to shout out an answer before the question was finished and the answer one shouted was usually not the correct one. Marsh's team protested, of course, but Mr. Reedy reprimanded Gilson's team only for the length of its questions, not the trickiness of them.

"That's part of the game," he said. "But so is the time limit for each round, so let's try to keep the questions within reasonable bounds."

Marsh felt somewhat like a train that has been derailed. He had been doing fine in the quiz. All that was required of him was that he listen alertly to the questions. While he was doing this, an unconscious process of connections would take place and in a flash he would find himself on the right track with the right answer on the tip of his tongue. Now Foster Gilson and his team had tampered with the switches and sent him off the track completely.

He comforted himself with the thought that it would all be a lot easier once he had learned the memory tricks Ellman had to teach him. Coming to the quiz with a memory like the one Ellman could give him would be like taking a test with an indexed volume of crib notes in his pocket.

Two world history texts, four paperback novels and, by way of experiment, a book on the theory and practice of accounting. It had taken Ellman more than an hour to select them. He paid for them, carried them home on the subway and put them on one of the big chairs in the living room.

It was this business of trying to select books for Marsh that brought home to Ellman how little he really knew or understood the boy. The biography of Tchaikovsky that had seemed so tempting to Ellman—it was the kind of book he would buy but never get around to reading, except in snippets now and then while the music was playing—would probably look like an uninviting bore to Marsh.

If he only knew what subjects interested Marsh. True, Mr. Berger had said that he did well in "technical" subjects at school, but Ellman did not really know what he meant by technical. He was afraid that he would only make a self-exposing blunder if he attempted to feed Marsh's interests along those lines. He could still recall a particularly painful birthday when a well-meaning aunt had presented him with a book on *The Art of Conversation*, presumably to help him with his stuttering.

He had toyed for a while with the idea of starting Marsh on one of his books on reading techniques, but eventually rejected that plan. He had a vision of Marsh quoting the book as an authority higher than Ellman himself and that would never do. Besides, the books would only confuse him, since each of them was constructed on the principle of learning by stages, whereas Ellman's idea of the way to learn was derived from the idea of "on the job" training. Throw it all at him at once and keep throwing it at him until he absorbs it. "He will learn by stages, but the stages will be determined by his own needs and abilities." For a while Ellman was lost in reflection on the difference between learning by stages and teaching by stages, but then he forced himself back to the matter at hand.

Chapter 14

When Marsh came up for his first lesson with Ellman, he was very conscious of the fact that it was Ellman, rather than any of the Bergers, who had suggested resuming the lessons. He wanted it quite clear from the very start just where they stood. He sat down, cleared his throat and said in a loud voice, "I came to learn memory and reading."

Ellman had disappeared into the bedroom.

"There is a book in front of you," he called.

Marsh looked. *Handbook of Radio Repair.* A thick hard-cover volume.

"Open it," Ellman commanded.

Marsh opened the book and looked at the flyleaf. The figure 15 was penciled inside the cover. The book was thick and swelled out, as though it had been left out in the rain.

"No," Ellman said, entering the room again. "Open it to the title page."

Marsh did so.

"Now," Ellman said. "Tear the page out."

By now Marsh knew Ellman well enough to know that anything was possible. Without hesitation he ripped the page out.

Ellman went into the kitchen and came back with a paper bag.

"Here," he said, unfolding the bag and shaking it open. "Put the paper in here."

Marsh deposited the paper in the bag and put the bag on the floor beside him.

"Now tell me," Ellman said. "What was on the page you just destroyed?"

Marsh felt that he had been fooled. He thought of the trick questions on the entrance exam. Maybe there was something on the other side of the title page that he was supposed to notice.

"Well, what was on the page?" Ellman asked again.

"Just the title," Marsh said.

"Right. But what *was* the title?"

"*Handbook of Radio Repair.*"

"Right again."

With a wave of the hand, Ellman cleared his mental blackboard.

"Now," he said, with his hand still raised in the air. "I want you to go through the whole book and do what you've just done. Glance at the page, get an idea of what it's about, and then rip it out and destroy it."

Marsh looked dolefully at the doomed book. He closed it, turned it over and opened it again from the back. One thousand and forty-two pages.

"I don't want you to *read* the book," Ellman said. "Just get an idea of what each page is about and as soon as you've got the idea then go on to the next page. There are chapter headings, bold print, diagrams, all kinds of things like that to help you."

Marsh turned to the first page again. He felt like a child, his breast swelling with a disappointed protest which he could not articulate. One thousand and forty-two pages. Divide that in half and it made more than five hundred pieces of paper to crumple up.

"Imagine you are trying to fix a radio," Ellman said. "Maybe that one you put together in your English composition. You know just what's wrong with it, but you're not sure how to fix it. So you get this book on radio repair. Only it doesn't have an index. So you have to thumb through it, looking for the item you want. You glance at each page. And if you know that it's *not* about the thing you are looking for, then you must have some idea in your mind of what it *is* about. And that is sufficient. At that point, you rip the page out and throw it away. It's very simple. The whole book shouldn't take you more than an hour."

Ellman set his watch on the table and Marsh settled into the book. It was more than a minute, however, before he even turned the first page.

"You should have turned at least ten pages by now," Ellman said. "What is the problem?"

"Well, this is the introduction. It's not about anything in particular."

"If you were looking something up, you'd just glance at the introduction long enough to see if it could tell you where to find it. That's all I want you to do. Just glance. Don't read."

Marsh ripped out the page he had been reading.

"In the introduction," Ellman went on, "just look at the first sentence of each paragraph to get the gist of what it's about."

Over the next ten minutes Marsh averaged only about four pages per minute. It was probably fast going for Marsh, but it was much slower than Ellman had expected.

"You're dawdling," Ellman said.

"I'm interested in something here."

"Good, but if you want to stay interested, you're going to have to keep moving along."

"But I want to *read* this part. I won't be able to come back to it later if I tear the book up."

"Right. This book is being used up. There are always plenty

151

of other books to look things up in if you must."

"But I'm *interested*," Marsh protested.

"Learn to read faster and you'll *widen* your range of interests," Ellman said. "That's what we're here for."

With an angry jerk, Marsh tore the page out.

"Marshall," Ellman said kindly. "That part you were just interested in. I don't know what it was, but I'd almost be willing to bet that it was something you were interested in before and just never looked up anywhere. Why not? Because looking things up usually involved a lot of careful reading and copying and studying. What we're trying to do now is to simplify all that clumsiness. If it helps, don't think of this as a course in how to read fast, think of it as a course in how to use books. Some are meant to be read quickly and others aren't. What you're developing is the skill to use each book in its own way."

Marsh sensed a small betrayal in that. Ellman was already making excuses, already telling Marsh in an indirect way that his dream of memorizing volumes at a glance was hopeless.

With a prod now and then from Ellman, Marsh was more than halfway through the book within an hour.

"We'll have to stop that now," Ellman said.

Marsh steadied himself for "Tell me all you can remember of what you've just read."

Ellman said, "Well, did you get anything out of it?"

"Yes," Marsh said. "It would have been better, though, if I could have really read it."

"Yes, but you *wouldn't* have read it. Even if you had started, you'd have given it up after ten pages."

Marsh grinned.

There was not enough book left to close. The front cover was now only a loose flap. Marsh folded this flap over the rest of the book and set it aside, expecting to resume with it at the next session.

"No, no," Ellman said. "Finish tearing it up. You don't have to do it page by page. Just rip it all up and throw it away. The book is all used up now anyway. One hour is all that's allowed."

The final destruction of the book took less than a minute. Ellman gave Marsh a few sheets of white paper and a pencil.

"I want you to make a couple of lists for me," he said.

"Is this for the memory?" Marsh asked.

Ellman smiled. "Yes," he said. "First I want you to make a list of all the books you can remember reading—especially the ones you had to make book reports on. Then I want you to make a list of all the television programs you watch, along with the day and time they're on—Sunday through Saturday. Third, give me a list of all the movie and television stars you can think of."

"I'll be here all night," Marsh said.

"Just do it for half an hour," Ellman said. "I want only as much as you can put down in that time."

Marsh was not really a regular television viewer. There were many programs, however, that he was familiar with because his parents watched them religiously and Marsh could hear them playing in the next room. He asked Ellman if he wanted programs like that on the list.

"If you're familiar with the content of the program, then include it on the list," the old man said.

But that led to another complication. If he was familiar with the content of two different programs that were on at the same day and time, should he include them both on the list? Donna was always talking about programs that his parents would not dream of watching, and sometimes Marsh watched them at her house.

"Put it all down," Ellman said. "Put down everything that comes into your head. If you have a question about some program, put the program down and write the question next to it."

Marsh decided that the lists were to be a memory exercise in themselves.

Courtney Callahan unpacked his new television set—a color portable with mirrormatic image, interlocking case and full visual sound—placed it on the table that had come with it and carefully rolled it into his clothes closet. He gathered up the wrappings and folded down the outside carton, with its bright MAGIC PLEX COLOR TV sign on it. Then he put on his coat and carried the wrappings with him as he left the house.

He walked two blocks and deposited them among the trash in front of someone else's house. The color television represented quite an investment to him and he saw no point in advertising to the world that he had it home now and ready for stealing.

Before returning to his room, he stopped in a candy store for a copy of *TV Guide*. Then he went into the hardware store and bought a can of white paint and a small brush.

The television set, to his relief, was still safely in the closet when he got home. He rolled the table over to the bed, turned the set over on its back and opened the paint.

In large block letters he printed the message on the bottom of the set: STOLEN FROM C. CALLAHAN 623 WEST 21ST ST.

The printing, even more than the exchange of money at the store, signified the purchase. The set was now unreturnably his. Even if it did not work, the store would not accept it back. This did not worry Callahan, however. If there was anything wrong with the set, he would raise holy hell all over the store until they agreed to fix it for him.

Two hundred and eighty-five dollars. He took a deep breath, plugged the set in, turned it on and sat back to see what his money had brought him.

The very first image he saw on his new set was the face of Porky Pig staring out through a rainbow while he stuttered, "Th-th-th-that's all, f-folks!"

The next day, Callahan called Ellman and invited him over to watch "Scholarship Quiz" with him.

"You may as well see what Marshall is in training for," he said.

"I can watch it here," Ellman said.

"Not in color," said Callahan.

"Another time," Ellman said.

"Why not now?"

"To be honest, I think I'm coming down with a cold. If I could go anywhere, I'd go to the bookstore to get some books for Marshall. As it is, I think I better stay in the house for a while."

"Wrap a scarf around your neck, put an overcoat on and come on over. You're not that old yet that a cold is the end of the world."

Ellman agreed to try it. "I'll come over to your place at about four o'clock."

The quiz program started at five. By four-thirty Ellman had still not arrived. Callahan put on his coat and went out to the corner to telephone him again.

"I'm sorry," Ellman said. "The cold is getting worse. I'd be foolhardy to go out now."

"Have you had a doctor?"

"What do I want a doctor for? It's just a cold. I thought I missed it this year but, just as winter is ending, it catches up with me."

"Are you taking anything for it?"

"Go home and watch the quiz," Ellman said.

"Okay, I will," Callahan said. "But after the quiz I'm coming down to your place. And if you won't tell me what you're using, I'll bring you what I take—Hydraine. It'll knock the cold right out of you."

Callahan had not seen any kind of quiz program since "$64,000 Question" went off the air. His first impression was one of awe at how hard everything had become. "What the hell is base two?" he found himself yelling at the television set.

Some of the questions were too involved to hold Callahan's interest to the end. The moderator began, "The premier of a newly independent East African republic whose name rhymes with the last name of a prominent French jurist recently declared . . ." and while Callahan was still trying to sort out the question one of the kids pushed his buzzer and shouted out a correct answer.

"Bolo!" Callahan repeated. "What would that be—the premier, the country, or the prominent French jurist?"

There were two questions, however, that Callahan felt he had some chance with. Both involved identifying a line of poetry. The first line was "If winter comes, can spring be far behind?" While Callahan was still snapping his fingers, a boy from East Chelsea High School identified it without hesitation as being from Shelley's "Ode to the West Wind."

Callahan, whose finger snaps were about to launch him into a recitation of "Roll on, thou deep and dark blue ocean roll," was quite impressed with this boy. He was not at all impressed with the boy from the opposing school who identified the line "tender is the night/ And haply the queen moon is on her throne . . ." Ever since Callahan's own school days, Keats' "Ode to a Nightingale" had been one of his special favorites.

"*Anybody* could have got that," he said.

After he had arrived at Ellman's, commented on how bad his cold seemed and forced him to swallow two Hydraine capsules, Callahan told him about the two boys.

"It's perfectly natural," Ellman said. "He knew something you didn't know and so you credited him with knowing *more* than you know."

"More about Shelley, anyway."

"That's the impression Marshall would like to create. The illusion of depth and wisdom. Like a magician in a vaudeville show, he doesn't really want to make things appear out of nowhere, only to be able to create the illusion that he can."

The second series of lessons had been going on for more than a month now. Ellman told Callahan about their first memory project.

"I made him associate various objects about the room with book titles," Ellman said. "The piano stool with the whirling seat was *Oliver Twist* and the table with the nicks in it was *Nicholas Nickleby*. Things like that. Then I asked him to close his eyes and mentally walk about the room naming off the books to me. He did it without a single mistake. When he finished I told him he had just named the complete works of Charles Dickens. He was amazed. 'I know all the works of Charles Dickens,' he said."

Callahan laughed.

"Yes," Ellman concluded. "He knew all of Dickens' works, but he had actually read only one of them. And all he could remember of that one was that Mr. Micawber used to keep saying that something will turn up."

Callahan suggested that Ellman interrupt the lessons for a while. "Give yourself a chance to get over this cold. It'd be a shame if you passed it on to Marshall and the cold kept him from being in the quiz."

"There are many things I intend to pass on to Marshall," Ellman said, "but my cold is not one of them."

After Callahan had left, Ellman stretched out on the bed and turned on the radio next to it. He wanted soft, soothing music to settle his brain. What he got was the *Scythian Suite*. He turned the dial but all that the other stations offered was rock music and news that for all its hot-off-the-wires freshness was still somehow stale to Ellman. He switched the radio off.

He was brain sick. That, at least, was one thing Callahan had been right about. "Ellman, you're driving yourself too hard," he had said.

Every moment of his waking life now was devoted to the new Marsh project. For each lesson he had to have three things prepared—a mnemonic for Marsh to learn, a subject on which he would ask Marsh to make a list, and a book for Marsh to read in an hour. Because Ellman was not able to get out to the bookstores, the books Marsh read now had to come from Ellman's own shelves. And each book had to be destroyed as fast as it was read.

The mnemonics required great skill on Ellman's part. He had joked with Callahan about the list of Dickens' works, but Ellman knew that these were the things that kept Marsh coming back to him. There was the list of Presidents he had included in the story beginning "Washington added Jefferson to the Mad Monster in Adam Jackson's Van when Harrison Tyler took a Polk at his Taylor and Fillmore Pierced Buchanan . . ." To rip a list like that out of context (what context was there for such a list—for any *list* for that matter?) and to deal with it purely as a sequence of sounds was a highly unintellectual way of manipulating symbols that at times frightened Ellman and at other times made him think himself quite brave.

The fear came during those moments when the unreality of what he was doing became real to him. The bravery came when he decided to go ahead in spite of the fear. Once he set a huge map of the world on the floor in the dead center of his apartment. Then he sectioned the apartment off into continents. Each room became a continent and each object of furniture in the room became a country in that continent.

It was easy to laugh at the idea that one of his battered old Grand Rapids chairs represented France, that his bookshelf was Greece, the piano was Italy and his television set was England. He was prepared for the sense of foolishness that he knew would come when he got down to the ludicrous particulars. It was having to go on in spite of the foolishness that caused the uncomfortable, diseased tingle in his spine. It was as though he could hear a faintly condescending voice ask, "You don't really *believe* all this, do you?"

Ellman's answer was to plunge even more deeply into the foolishness. The bed was China, the table next to it was Japan and the radio he had just turned off was India. Straight-faced foolishness gave way to stark unreality and Ellman had no doubt that his present cold was the result of the strain he had put himself through. He strengthened himself with the thought that Marsh, at least, would be spared the mind-boggling job of creating it all. His task would simply be to look about him and make the prepared associations. Once he had the countries associated with the furniture, he would not only be able to rattle off a list of countries, but he would also have a solid object representing that country to which he could attach a whole series of associations.

That was what most appealed to Ellman—the idea that these associations were something he could build on. A series of disconnected news items about some given country could be artificially associated with the object representing that country. In time the news items themselves would begin to tie together, to help Marsh form some solid idea of the country itself. Then the artificial associations would drop away and real knowledge would begin.

What he could do with geographical space Ellman felt he could also do with time. That was another project that was wearying his brain and taxing his strength—the chronology. He had broken the week up into periods in American history. Sunday was the Age of Exploration and Colonization, and the list of Sunday-night television programs that Marsh had written out for him had become a series of associations with people and events of that period. Ellman had sat glued to the television set for a week, going from his history book to his notebook and scribbling associations as fast as he could think them up.

It did not bother him that the Civil War occurred in the midst of a situation comedy or that the Great Depression was woven into the fabric of a husband-and-wife quiz program. By now he was used to these incongruities and could even persuade himself that they were assets. The important thing was that he had been able to superimpose a sequence of events that Marsh had not been able to retain on top of a sequence that he had already retained without effort. All that was necessary for him now was to take Marsh through the series of associations and drill him in them a couple of times.

Ellman rolled over and turned the radio on again. He no longer cared how stale the news was or how noisy the music. He needed something outside himself to rest his thoughts on. Anything would do.

Chapter 15

Every time that Marsh decided he was wasting his time with Ellman, something would happen that made him want to hold on a bit longer. The result of all the list-making he did was that Marsh constantly found himself making lists on his own. Things always came to his head in clusters, and even the reading project had been more of a success than Marsh had at first realized.

Ellman paced him through a biography of Napoleon one night, rapping the table every twenty seconds as a sign that Marsh was to turn the page. Thinking about it the next day, Marsh did not really feel that he had read the book at all, and yet—there was always an "and yet" where Ellman was concerned—he had to admit the next day that he knew more about the book, and about Napoleon, than he had before he had begun reading.

Ellman had divided his apartment into continents and countries. Without telling Ellman, Marsh adapted this idea to his own uses, dividing his own apartment into historical periods. The bathroom represented the Prehistoric Age. The four corners of his parents' bedroom were Egypt, Babylon, Greece and Rome. His own bedroom accommodated the Middle Ages, the Renaissance and the Age of Exploration and Discovery. The Industrial Revolution and the Nineteenth Century were crowded together in the kitchen. The Twentieth Century was the living room. Much of Marsh's spare time was spent making up lists of things to connect with this structure.

At one session Ellman gave him a list of the names of "Great Philosophers" in chronological order of birth, to be memorized by a "knitwork" method that Ellman had taught him—associating each item on the list with the item following. Marsh asked if he could have the dates for each one.

"You don't have to memorize dates now," Ellman said. "That's a numbers code. We'll get on to that later."

"I want the dates anyway," Marsh said. "Just to get an idea."

Ellman was pleased and gave Marsh the dates. Marsh, having memorized the names, spent some extra time placing the philosophers in their appropriate place in his apartment.

Ellman began the next session by asking Marsh how much he remembered from the philosophers list. Only two names escaped him—Swedenborg and Nietzsche. Then Ellman produced the volume Marsh was to "read" that night—*Lives of the Great Philosophers.*

"We may as well tie it all in," Ellman said.

Marsh was puzzled for a long time about the lists he had to make up himself. One evening he had to write down the names of all the baseball players he could remember, and on another evening he had to list as many different things he could think of that were made of glass. At first he thought that Ellman was going to organize these lists and give them back to Marsh to rememorize in a more logical order. Then for a while he expected Ellman to use the lists in one of his "knitwork" associations. But so far none of these things had happened. After that he figured that the lists must be some kind of a test—to see how many things could pop into his head at the same time. But he could not imagine how such a test could be graded.

The answer came to him in an oblique way, vaguely associated with the answer to a question Mr. Reedy asked him at quiz practice one day. The question itself had to do with the chemical formula for hydrofluoric acid. Marsh did not have the answer at his fingertips, so he set himself to think about it. And the grid of his mind as he waited for the answer, silent and expectant, was the same as when he was making up a list. The difference between the two situations was that in the quiz he was looking for a specific item while in the list-making he was waiting for one of many things. But in both cases he was simply waiting for the conscious appearance of something that he knew must be in his brain somewhere.

The list-making, then, was a form of practicing for the quiz —a way of making the things that were in his brain available to him when he wanted them. It was a way of greasing the engine, splicing the cables, soldering the wires.

At the end of the quiz session during which Marsh made this discovery, Mr. Reedy announced the date on which the team would make its debut on television.

"The program is taped on a Wednesday," he said. "We are scheduled for the Wednesday after next, which is less than two weeks away."

"What school do we go up against?" Kite asked.

"Our opponents will be a team from the Tessi School."

"Tessy who?"

This brought great laughter, which Mr. Reedy put down with a frown and a shake of his head.

"It's a private school and a very good one," he said grimly. "And it's all girls."

This announcement brought a mixed reaction. Before the boys could get into a discussion of the mixture, Mr. Reedy put on his "official" voice again and brought them to quiet attention.

"Next Friday afternoon in the school auditorium we are going to have a full-dress rehearsal for the quiz. The entire student body will be present. So may any of your parents, friends or relatives who care to come."

There was a lot of "this is it" murmuring. In the midst of it all, Marsh raised his hand.

"Who is going to make up the questions for the dress rehearsal?" he asked.

Mr. Reedy smiled. "The faculty will be responsible for the questions," he said. "But we are going to give the students a chance too. On Monday every student in the school will be asked to submit five questions. We may use these on Friday."

"A week from Wednesday!" Mrs. Berger said. "I knew you should have got the suit last weekend. We'll go tomorrow."

Mr. Berger said that he would not be able to get away from work for the dress rehearsal.

"You're gonna ask Ellman too, right?" he asked Marsh.

"Sure. Anyway, I'll tell him when it is and if he wants to come, he's welcome."

"Tell him I'm bringing my sister," Mrs. Berger said. "And I have to go over to her house that morning and from there straight to the school."

Mr. Berger said nothing and his expression did not change. Nevertheless, Mrs. Berger interpreted his silence as an objection.

"I don't care," she added. "This is a big thing for me as well as Marsh and I'm not going to have *him* spoiling the enjoyment."

When Marsh told Ellman of the dress rehearsal, Ellman received the information but did not seem to realize that it was also an invitation.

"You can come if you want to," Marsh said. "You might like it."

"If my cold is better," Ellman said.

Ellman's cold had hung on for so long already that Marsh

had some doubt that he would ever get over it, but he said nothing.

Each night Callahan had called Ellman to see if he needed anything and each night Ellman assured him that he was fine, it was no trouble for him to go down to the grocery on the corner once a day and anyway he had lots of canned goods in the house. Then on Saturday Callahan came by himself and was appalled by what he found.

"You look terrible," he said. "What the hell have you been doing?"

"Nothing," Ellman said. "I sit at the table, consult a few books, make some notes, prepare a lesson for Marshall."

Callahan shook his head. "In other words, you rack your brains and wear yourself out just so you can make it easy for him."

"That's not true," Ellman said.

"Ellman, you have a cold. You should be resting. You keep driving yourself like this and you'll never get over it. At your age even a cold can be something serious."

"You said just the opposite when you wanted me to go to your house. Then a cold was nothing to worry about."

"If it wasn't serious, it wouldn't have held on like this."

Callahan walked to the corner where the bookshelf stood.

"Look," he said. "Books on the floor, books on the chair, books on the table. You're all over the place working."

Ellman laughed. "I was rearranging the bookshelf just before you came in. That's why the books are spread around like that."

"That's your idea of taking it easy?"

Ellman sat down.

"All right," he said. "I'll take it easy. And if it makes you feel any better, I'll point out that the cold is gone. I'm not sneezing anymore. I'm coughing now."

After commenting on the scarf wrapped around his neck and the "healthy sound" of the deep cough that Ellman let out, Callahan let himself be led into recounting some of the latest post office gossip, bringing Ellman up to date on the doings of everyone at the station whom he still remembered. He noticed, though, that while he was speaking Ellman's eyes rarely left the pile of books on the floor. The old man's expression was thoughtful but static, more like that of a person in a trance than of one who is actively working out a problem.

"As soon as I leave you're going to get right back at those books, aren't you?" Callahan said with resignation.

"No," Ellman said. He shook the thoughtful expression off his face and pointed his chin at the ceiling. "At any rate, there isn't much to do now. It's only a matter of putting them back on the shelf."

Callahan walked to the shelf and picked up a stack from the floor.

"Okay," he said. "What goes where?"

Ellman protested, but Callahan pointed out that he would have no peace of mind now until the stacking was finished, so Ellman directed him through the process.

In the midst of giving directions, Ellman was seized by a coughing fit. He went into the bedroom to take some cough medicine. Before he returned to the living room Callahan had finished his task.

There were two feet of empty space after the last book on the bottom shelf.

"I used to have to keep some books on that end table over there," he said to Callahan, "because there wasn't room for them on the shelf. Now there's plenty of room."

Without waiting to be asked, he told Callahan about the reading program he had undertaken with Marsh.

"As I couldn't get to the stores, I had to 'cannibalize' my own library."

"Why didn't you tell Marshall to bring his own books?"

"Because he would have bought cheap books, not worth reading."

"You could have told him what books to bring."

"Too much trouble and expense to get them."

"Hell!" Callahan exploded. "It's all for him anyway, isn't it? Let him have some of the bother."

"No," Ellman said. "It wasn't all for him. Some of it was for me. Most of it, I think."

Something in the tone of Ellman's voice made Callahan latch onto the word "was."

"Does that mean you're going to call it quits after all?" he asked.

"It's going to end soon anyway," Ellman said. "Week after next is the quiz. Once that starts, the lessons are over."

"Are you sure of that?"

"Of course. The quiz is all the incentive Marshall has. Once it starts, there won't be time for any more lessons."

They sat in silence for a while and then Callahan remembered a hockey game that was being televised that afternoon, so they turned on the set. Neither of them was much of a sports spectator, but hockey was at least a fast-moving game and they got some enjoyment out of it.

After the game Callahan announced that he was staying for dinner.

"Where's that grocery store you talk about? I'll get some frankfurters and a can of sauerkraut."

Ellman clutched the wool scarf around his neck. "I don't think sauerkraut," he said.

"How about beans?" Callahan said. "I'll get the kind they put honey in. That'd be good for your throat."

"Just a TV dinner will do for me," Ellman said. "Any kind. I'll have a can of soup with it."

Callahan stood in the doorway.

"Are those TV dinners any good?" he asked.

"Only when you have a cold. Then *everything* is tasteless."

Callahan brought back two frozen roast beef dinners.

"It'll probably be just as bad as they say," he told Ellman while the dinners were heating. "But I figure I ought to try one at least once."

Callahan's first comment was that the food was "too hot." When he finished, his summation was, "It's not as bad as they say. I've tasted a lot worse in my time, let me tell you. A lot worse."

"It's edible and inoffensive," Ellman said. "That's the best that can be said for it. The only thing you can resent about it is that it has the arrogance to try and pass itself off as food. Just as these mnemonics try and pass themselves off as learning."

"You have a one-track mind."

"It eats at me," Ellman said. "The more bits and pieces of superficial knowledge I stuff into Marshall's head, the more aware I become of how ignorant he really is. 'How limited his range, how shallow his grasp.'"

"You're quoting?"

"Quoting myself. Marshall can recite the Presidents of the United States with all the authority of an expert historian and only I know the trivia that goes through his mind while he speaks the names." Ellman raised his voice in a wail of resentment. "Washington added Jefferson to the Mad Monster!"

Callahan laughed.

"I give him the image of intelligence, the trappings of scholarship. He can recite dozens of lists and identify books and authors and even quote lines of poetry. And do you know what I feel when I listen to him? Do you know what satisfaction and gratification there is in it?"

"What?"

"None. I feel as though I had spoken these things into a tape recorder and I was playing back the recording. I wanted to be a teacher. If you record something on tape, have you taught the machine something? Can you take pride in that?"

Callahan protested that Ellman was being unfair. "It's the cold talking," he said. "You're sick and tired." Callahan smiled as if he had stumbled on a joke. "You're not sick and tired of teaching, you're just plain sick and tired."

"I haven't been teaching," Ellman said. "I've been painting scenery. Putting up a fine facade for Marshall. Marshall knows the names of all the 'Great Painters' although he has never spent more than ten seconds looking at a picture in his life unless it was something in a sex magazine."

"Marshall reads books like that?"

"He knows the names of the Great Composers, Poets, Writers and Philosophers, although all he knows of their work is what he can absorb from simplified synopses. That's good enough for me, but Marshall is setting out to pass himself off as an educated man. It is not good enough for him."

"He hasn't even started college yet," Callahan said. "Give him a chance. In grammar school you memorize, in high school you work and in college you think."

"I've seen that he was exposed to information," Ellman said. "But I haven't been able to give him experience. It's ironic that he came to me in the first place to learn history. You don't learn history, you experience it."

"In Moslem countries," Callahan said, "kids have to learn the Koran by heart. That's the whole of their education. Learning the Koran word for word."

Ellman stared blankly at Callahan. Callahan smiled. Ellman laughed. Nothing more was said about Marsh until after dinner when Callahan remembered that it was Saturday and they had forgotten to watch the quiz. Ellman said he had not forgotten it. He just did not want to see it.

"My brother Jacob used to tell about an old operatic movie he had seen once. He was never able to tell who was in it or who produced it, so I always suspected that the movie existed only in his own imagination. It was about the early struggles of a tenor. Moving freight in Naples, singing along the canals of Venice in the best movie style, and being heard by a famous impresario who declares him to have the greatest natural voice since Caruso. The impresario sends him to a great teacher and there is a montage of scales and training. Then a debut with a local opera company in front of an audience that comes cheering to its feet after *'Che gelida manina.'* Then a series of arias and excerpts as he tours the provinces singing with local companies. Finally the big night. His debut at the Grand Opera House before the cream of society and the leading lights of the musical world. The opera is *Carmen* and he is singing Don José. The Carmen is an established star, another student of the great teacher, who comes to his dressing room before the performance to wish him well. The moment of solitude in the dressing room before the curtain goes up when he says his 'Hail Mary' and crosses himself. Then the first act, which brings some strong applause even for the insipid *'Parlez-moi de ma mère'* duet, during which he receives strong support from the soprano who plays Micaela. And at last the moment of triumph, the second-act aria *'La fleur que tu m'avais jetée,'* which brings the audience to its feet with applause.

"The film should have ended there, of course, but it continues through the next scene of the opera. The tenor is backstage being congratulated by his manager and making plans for his future. Alone on the stage, Micaela, played by a soprano who is also making her debut that evening, has begun the aria *'Je dis que rien ne m'épouvante.'* At first it is almost impossible to hear her amid the hubbub in the tenor's dressing room. But the camera comes in close on the tenor as he becomes aware of the sound drifting from the stage. A strange light comes into his eyes. 'Listen,' he says, and gradually the others around him become quiet. He opens the door of the dressing room and as he approaches the wings, the sound of her voice fills the theater. No one is moving backstage. All stand transfixed, listening. As the aria ends, there is a moment of silence. Then a torrent of applause breaks from the theater. Everyone in the gallery rises to his feet with shouts of 'Bravo' and 'Encore.' The demonstration is noisier and deeper than the one given to the tenor. And the clamor ends only when the soprano, in a move unprecedented in that opera house, is forced to repeat the entire aria from the beginning. Clearly the night is *her* night. And that is the way the picture ends."

Ellman smiled as he finished the story. Callahan smiled back at him. Ellman seemed to think the point of the story was perfectly obvious, but the truth was that Callahan was not sure whether it was intended to deepen his knowledge of Marsh, of Ellman's brother Jacob, or of Julius Ellman himself.

Until Sunday night Marsh's weekend was great. On Friday night Donna's parents went out, so he and Donna had the apartment to themselves to relax their nerves in. On Saturday he watched the quiz and, using one of Ellman's methods memorized all the questions. Saturday night there was a free-for-all party at Danny Lensman's to take his mind off his troubles, and on Sunday afternoon he astonished his parents by memorizing all the questions asked during a television interview with the Secretary of Defense and giving them a summary of the interview as soon as the program went off the air. His mother immediately foresaw a great future for him as a television commentator and his father, trying to get behind the scenes, kept saying, "I don't know how that trick works but whatever the trick is, it's a damned good one."

Sunday night he went to a movie with Donna. After the movie they went to a restaurant for hamburgers and Coke.

They sat at the counter. After Marsh had given their order, he asked Donna if she had watched "Ask the Man" on television that afternoon.

"Are you kidding?" Donna asked.

"It was really good, more interesting than you think. They had the Secretary of Defense on. They were asking him questions and while they did I was memorizing the questions by the classification chain system—"

"Will you cut it out?" Donna said.

"Cut what out?"

"You're getting to be a real pain with your 'I memorized this' and 'I memorized that.' So what? I mean who cares?"

"I care. The Secretary of Defense is on TV so I watch him. Are you telling me I'm not supposed to take an interest in what goes on in the world?"

"You don't take any more interest in what goes on in the world than I do. You just want everyone to think you have a big brain."

"The bigger they are, the harder they fall."

"What's that supposed to mean?"

"I don't know. It just popped into my head."

Donna snorted. "The bigger the head, the harder the rocks," she said. "And I don't know what that means, either."

The waitress brought their order.

"Seriously," Marsh said, "do you think I overdo it?"

"Overdo isn't the word," Donna said. "And then last night at Danny's party when you wanted to turn off the stereo and play quiz program, for God's sake."

Marsh slapped the counter. "I was kidding," he said. "How many times do I have to tell you that?"

"Well, you're the only one that knows you were kidding. Everybody else thought you were serious. Honestly, I was embarrassed for you."

"I don't want to talk about it."

"I think you should. Those damned lessons are going to your head in more ways than one."

"Will you shut up?"

"Don't tell me to shut up," Donna said. "I'll talk as much as I want to."

They had been talking in subdued tones, so as not to be overheard by the waitress or the other patrons. Marsh swallowed a bite of his hamburger and then in the same restrained voice asked, "How are things going at the job?"

Donna laughed. "What's this, change-the-subject time?" she asked.

"You told me you expected to get fired. I was wondering if it happened yet."

"You think if I got fired you'd have to *ask* me about it?"

"I was just making conversation."

"You want conversation? I'll give you conversation. When are you going to quit those damned lessons?"

Marsh gave her an angry glare. Donna threw her hands up in the air and stared piously at the ceiling. "God protect me," she said. "I mentioned the sacred subject."

"You know everybody's looking over here, don't you?"

Donna glared at the waitress, who was looking at them from the other end of the counter. "They probably think I'm trying to seduce you," she said.

Donna was pleased and started to laugh at her own joke, but Marsh did not join her in the laugh.

"All right," Marsh said. "I'll give it to you straight. I don't care what you, Danny or anybody else thinks. I get more out of those lessons than I do out of the schoolwork or anything else. They give me a way to make sense out of everything and I'm not giving them up. Not for anything."

Chapter 16

On Monday they went directly into the book without any mnemonic or any review of the previous week's work. The book was H. G. Wells' *Outline of History* and Marsh was fascinated to see so many people and periods flash in front of his eyes so quickly. At first he thought he was going faster than the agreed-on speed of ten pages per minute, but when he checked it against his watch, he found that Ellman was not keeping the pace accurately. Apparently he had his mind on other things.

After the book, Ellman set Marsh to writing down the titles of all the songs to which he could remember the tunes. There were few moments during the course of the next half hour during which Marsh was not wielding his pen in total absorption.

"All of these are songs? Popular songs?" Ellman said when he read the list.

"Sure," Marsh said. "One time or another, they've all been in the top twenty."

"Out of the whole list I see only one I recognize."

Marsh smiled. "Probably a revival."

Ellman put the list away.

"I never realized how many songs I knew," Marsh said. "And I wasn't even warming up when it was time to stop.

Imagine if the words were chemical formulas and mathematical theorems instead of love. I'd have it all right there at my finger tips."

"If the lyrics were all chemical formulas and mathematical theorems," Ellman pointed out, "you'd very quickly lose whatever interest you had in popular music."

"It's a good idea, though."

If it was, it was nevertheless one that Ellman did not wish to dwell on.

"Marshall," he said. "I know the quiz is coming up next week and you undoubtedly have a lot of work to do preparing for it. I was wondering, then, if you might not want to end the lessons now instead of waiting until next week."

"End the lessons?" Marsh said. "Why?"

"You've got the dress rehearsal on Friday and the television quiz next Wednesday. You don't want to get yourself all keyed up working right down to the last minute."

"You mean this is the end?" Marsh said. "I don't understand."

"Marshall, the quiz starts next week. For the little bit you'd gain in the few extra lessons—"

"What's the quiz got to do with it?" Marsh said. "I thought it was supposed to help me with the college work. You were going to teach me to read a book in a flash and to memorize things in nothing flat. I'm only just beginning to get the hang of it. You can't quit now."

"Marshall, I'm not well. I have a cough."

"All right, so we'll skip this week's lesson and next week when you feel better we'll start up again."

"*If* I feel better."

"It's only a cough," Marsh said, trying to make the words sound comforting rather than callous. "You'll get over it."

Ellman looked for a moment as though he were going to argue with Marsh, but he checked himself. He glanced about the room, from the television set to the bookshelf, and then sat heavily in one of the hard chairs at the table.

"Marshall," he said. "I don't think you understand how much preparation goes into all this, how much strain it takes to prepare a mnemonic, how much time it takes to select just the right books. And those books you tear up, they don't come free, you know. They cost money."

"I don't have to tear them up," Marsh said.

"Yes you do. Forget I said that about them costing money. Some of them I've had for years without even bothering to read them myself. I doubt if I could get ten dollars for the whole lot of them from a secondhand dealer."

Ellman momentarily ran out of words. Restlessly he shuffled the notebooks and papers in front of him, as if seeking inspiration from them.

"What I'm saying is that it's not as easy as it seems to teach, to prepare lessons, to guide a young mind. I'm not even sure I'm qualified to do it."

"You said you could."

"Maybe I was biting off more than I could chew. Maybe it was too late in life for me to start a project like this. Maybe it would *never* have worked."

"But it *is* working," Marsh said.

"In what way, at what cost? You don't know the strain it's putting on me, the effort it takes. And I don't know the effect it's having on you. The long-term effects, I mean. Your approach to things, your attitude."

"I know more than I ever knew before. I'm interested in things I never understood before. I read more."

Ellman stood up and turned his back to Marsh.

"You can't quit cold like this," Marsh said with heavy wisdom. "It's not fair."

Ellman stared at the wall for a long time. Then he turned around and looked Marsh straight in the eye.

"The geographic mnemonic," he said. "Do you know how long it took me to work that out? Pacing up and down this apartment, assigning and reassigning names? Days. It took me at least three days and at the end of those days I felt as if I'd moved a whole mountain by carrying away one wheelbarrow of dirt at a time."

"The Emperor of Ethiopia was in Washington last week. I know more about his country than anybody else in my class. Including the guy who's always yelling about Black Studies."

"The key-word chain that we used to memorize the outline for the Constitution. It took me nearly a week to work that out."

"And I'll bet you know more about the Constitution now than you ever did before. I know I do. And I'll never forget it, either."

"Yes, but have you ever actually read the Constitution from beginning to end?"

"I skimmed through it the day after I memorized the outline. I didn't want to read it the way I used to read things before because I was afraid it would be bad practice."

Ellman was genuinely surprised. He sat down at the table again.

"You never told me this," he said.

Marsh shrugged. "Am I supposed to tell you everything?" he asked.

Ellman rose and paced about the room like someone forced to make a difficult decision in a short time.

"No!" he said, turning to Marsh and raising both hands in the air. "Whether I want to or not, I simply can't."

Marsh did not have to ask what he was referring to. "Instead of working out the mnemonics yourself," he said, "why can't we work them out together? I've already done a few of my own. You could show me a few extra tricks. I'm supposed to learn to do it on my own anyway. That's what it's all about, right?"

Marsh told Ellman about his division of his own apartment into periods of world history and Ellman, hearing the siren song, fought down the temptation to tell Marsh about his own American history version of the television schedule.

"That's very good, Marshall," he said. "But don't you see what it means? You don't need me anymore. You can do it now yourself."

"There's more to it and you know it. I need you. Not only to help me work things out but to make me stick to it."

Marsh rose to his feet and moved decisively to the door.

"You're tired now," he said. "You have a cold. So no more lessons this week. I won't come back until Monday and we'll work out a new schedule then."

"That's your problem," Callahan shouted into the phone. "My problem is keeping the platform clear."

"My truck driver doesn't come back to the shop after his rounds are done," the voice on the telephone said. "I can't pick it up. Don't you understand that?"

"Your weight is off. We can't accept the mail and I want it off the platform and out of here by tonight."

"Callahan, if it was anybody but you, I'd offer him ten bucks and that'd be the end of it."

Callahan snorted. "If it was anybody but you I'd probably take it," he said, slamming the phone down.

He had barely time enough to let out a few choice words before the phone rang again.

"Weigh section," he shouted, picking it up. "Callahan speaking."

"Callahan? Ellman speaking."

"How are you?"

"You sound like they're giving you a bad time up there."

Callahan tried to take the acid out of his voice. "One of those days," he said.

Ellman told him he wanted to discuss something with him and that if Callahan would be home that evening he would come by his room.

"Don't be foolish," Callahan said. "You can't be all that much over your cold yet. If you want to talk to me I'll come to your place."

When Callahan arrived, Ellman told him of his conversation with Marsh.

"He acted as though I were the student and he the teacher, treating me like a child that didn't know its own mind."

"Well, *do* you?" Callahan said. "It seems to me that if you really wanted to end the lessons, all you'd have to do is say no and stick to it."

"You don't know what it's like," Ellman said. "I'd have his father up here. How many times can you say no?"

"As often as you have to."

Callahan went to the front window and looked out.

"Nothing to see but the windows across the street," Ellman said. "Marshall told me once that he knew the people directly across the street and right away I started trying to figure out a way to put a face in each window and use the facade of the building, with its windows and faces, as a means to memorize some sort of a chart or diagram."

"Everything is grist for the mill, huh?"

"It's an obsession," Ellman said. "Come away from the window."

Ellman sat in the chair under the lamp. Taking the other armchair, Callahan studied his friend's face and saw that even though the cold symptoms had faded and Ellman was returning to equilibrium, he was not the same Ellman he had been before. There was something new in his face now that Callahan believed would remain with him for the rest of his life—a flatness, a glazed look about the eyes. In some way the old man had really become an old man at last.

"You've been talking to me in much the same way Marshall did," Ellman said. "And I suppose I deserve it. If you act like a child, you deserve to be treated like a child."

"No one said you were acting like a child," Callahan said.

"*I* say it," Ellman said. "For years now I've been saying that I wanted to be a teacher. It seemed to me to be the greatest thing in the world. I felt that if I had the opportunity I could turn anyone in the world into a genius. Instead I find that my ideas of 'genius' are every bit as superficial as Marshall's."

"I don't want to listen to this," Callahan said, getting to his feet. "You've been good for Marshall. Everything proves it."

"I have been good for Marshall. I admit that. I claim it, in fact. But I've done everything I can for him. Callahan, you're supposed to be the practical one. When I tell you I'm at my wits' end, I mean it. I would have been a good teacher once, but it's too late now, especially in an arrangement like this where there's no end to it."

"Set an end to it. To the end of the school term or the end of the summer."

"You don't understand. It was an illusion and I've seen through it. I want to get out of it. Now!"

"Then what's the problem?"

"Marshall. I owe him something."

"You did plenty for Marshall already. You don't owe him anything."

"I did no more for Marshall than any of these books could have done by themselves if he'd only taken the time to study them."

Ellman walked to the shelf and started pulling out books and calling off titles. "*The Key to the Mind, One Hundred Memory Tricks, Reading Up a Storm, The Magic Memory Book.*" Ellman turned to Callahan. "Almost everything I've done with Marshall I've drawn from these books," he said. "The same books that kept my own foolish daydream alive so long."

"Then there's your answer," said Callahan.

"What?"

"Give him the books."

Ellman was speechless at the simplicity of it.

"Get rid of the daydream and the books and do something for Marshall all at the same time," Callahan said. "You don't have to explain anything to him. Just tell him you're too tired to go on but give him the books to help himself with and let it go at that."

"Good," Ellman said. "But the business about being tired—Marshall would never understand that. I'll speak to his father Friday at the dress rehearsal."

Chapter 17

Mrs. Berger's sister's daughter was sick on the day of Marsh's dress rehearsal. Consequently she had to stay home from school. Consequently her mother had to stay with her. Consequently Mrs. Berger had to go to Marsh's triumph alone.

She set the house to rights as soon as her husband had left for work. Then she had a long bath, after which she relaxed in front of the television for a while. At eleven-thirty she began to dress and by twelve-thirty she was all ready. Which meant that she could watch two more of her stories on television.

At one-thirty sharp she turned the television off, put her coat and hat on and looked around, giving the house a parting check. The windows were locked, all the lights were out, no water was running and the gas range was not lit. All was well.

She walked very quietly and slowly down the stairs, fearful that she might run into Ellman at every turn and yet angry at herself for being afraid. If I see him, she told herself, I'll just tell him I'm on my way to my sister's and that's it. It's bad enough he's got me sneaking out of my own house like a thief. I don't want him following me all the way to the school too.

She did not want to delay any longer than she had to, but it was second nature with Mrs. Berger to glance at the mailbox every time she passed through the vestibule. There was mail there and even though she felt sure it must be all bills and advertisements, she knew she would have no peace until she had looked through it. Three bills, a copy of *TV Guide* and a letter for Marsh from City College.

Quickly Mrs. Berger stuck the magazine back into the mailbox and the bills into her purse. Without hesitation she ripped open Marsh's letter.

Marsh had been accepted as a student and would be notified later of the date of registration for classes.

Mrs. Berger's first impulse was to run back upstairs and telephone her sister, but she knew that if she got involved in phone calls she would never make it to the school in time for the quiz. Besides, the one who had the most right to know was Marsh. Stuffing the letter into her purse with the bills, she walked briskly in the direction of the bus stop.

At the corner she met Mrs. Corcoran, who was coming out of the grocery store.

"What are you all dolled up for?" Mrs. Corcoran asked.

Mrs. Corcoran was the answer to a prayer.

"My Marsh was accepted at the City College," Mrs. Berger said. "I'm going up to the school now to see him in a quiz. I'm late now so I have to hurry."

Mrs. Corcoran waved her on. "Congratulations," she called after her. "Have a good time."

The center rows of the orchestra were reserved for the students. They were already in their places when Mrs. Berger arrived at the school. The side aisles were for parents and friends. Mr. Reedy was standing at the back of the auditorium. Mrs. Berger knew him from parents' night and went directly up to speak to him.

"You don't recognize me," she said, "but I'm Mrs. Berger, Marsh's mother. You're Mr. Reedy, aren't you?"

"Yes."

At that moment Mrs. Berger felt a pull at her elbow. She ignored it.

"Where is Marsh?" she asked Mr. Reedy. "I have something important to tell him."

Instead of answering, Mr. Reedy cast a curious glance over her shoulder while Mrs. Berger felt another pull at her elbow. She turned, expecting to see Marsh behind her.

It was Ellman.

"I've been calling you ever since I saw you come in," he said. "Where is Mr. Berger?"

"He's not here," she said curtly. She turned once more to Mr. Reedy. "I have to see Marsh. I got a letter for him," she said.

"Marsh is backstage right now getting ready for the quiz. Unless it's something very urgent, I don't think we ought to take the chance of upsetting him right now."

"He got accepted by City College," Mrs. Berger said proudly. She began reaching in her purse and, as she did so, Ellman tapped once more at her elbow.

"I'm with friends," she said, without raising her eyes from the purse. "They're holding a seat for me on the side. It's on the aisle. Just one seat."

"Will Mr. Berger be here later?" Ellman asked.

"He had to go to work today," she said, looking up at him. "He won't be able to make it."

Ellman hesitated a moment and Mrs. Berger went back to burrowing in her bag. If he *had* to talk to her, she asked herself between clenched teeth, did it *have* to be right in front of Marsh's teacher?

She pulled out the letter.

"Would you tell him I'd like to see him tonight when he comes home?" Ellman said. "It's about the—"

Mrs. Berger waved the letter in Ellman's face. "Marsh got accepted at City College," she said.

"That's wonderful," Ellman said. "But of course I never doubted that he would be accepted."

"I don't think news like that will upset him," Mr. Reedy put in. "On the contrary. If you like, I'll take the letter backstage and give it to him myself before the quiz starts. It might boost his confidence."

Mrs. Berger held the letter tightly in her hand.

"You want to give it to him yourself," Mr. Reedy said understandingly.

"It's about the lessons," Ellman interrupted. "Tell Mr. Berger—"

"What lessons?" Mrs. Berger said, rounding on Ellman. "I don't know anything about any lessons."

"The reading lessons, the memory—"

"They don't discuss any of that stuff with me and I don't know what you're talking about."

She turned to Mr. Reedy once more. "I'll see Marsh after and give him the letter then."

Mr. Reedy's eyes were following Ellman, who was slowly moving off toward one of the aisles of the auditorium.

"That's the man who lives upstairs in our building," Mrs. Berger said angrily. "He's always butting in on other people's business."

Mr. Reedy returned his attention to Mrs. Berger.

"You don't want me to tell Marsh then?" he asked.

Mrs. Berger was still holding the college letter in her hand. With a gesture that was almost like throwing it away, she pressed the letter on the teacher.

"Oh, give it to him," she said lifelessly. "Tell him. What difference does it make?"

Marsh was somewhat surprised to discover that the contestants in the quiz had to wear makeup. They would need it, they were told, for the television cameras and since they wanted the dress rehearsal to be as much like the real thing as possible, makeup would be required this afternoon also.

"This way they'll be able to see you clearly in the back row," Miss Turner, the home economics teacher, explained as she made him up.

To Marsh, the makeup added to the sense of unreality he was feeling. First his face had to be painted in a certain way and then his mind had to be set in a certain grid. In a way, the makeup made him feel free to be as phony, as hair-splitting and as obtrusively knowledgeable as he was capable of being. It would not be his real self sitting up there on the stage, only his made-up public self, his trained self, his hair-trigger memory and steel-trap brain. Marsh smiled, called it nerves and tried to relax.

In Marsh's present frame of mind, the decision to smile had all the force of a posthypnotic suggestion. The smile became printed on his face like the makeup and remained there long after he had forgotten about it. He was still smiling when Mr. Reedy approached him carrying an envelope in his hand.

"I met your mother outside," the teacher explained. "She asked me to give you this."

Marsh's hand shook slightly as he reached for the envelope and recognized the return address. She wouldn't have sent it to him now if it meant failure, he reasoned. But then, on the other hand, if it meant success she would surely have wanted to tell him herself.

He read the letter.

"I've been accepted!" he said.

"I know," Mr. Reedy said. "Congratulations."

Marsh carefully put the letter back into the envelope and then tucked the envelope into his side pocket.

"If you don't mind," Mr. Reedy said, "I'd just as soon you didn't go out on stage with an envelope sticking out of your pocket. I'll hold it for you."

"I can fold it in half."

"No bulging pockets allowed, either," Mr. Reedy said. "I'll take it."

Marsh grinned and handed over the letter. Mr. Reedy looked at his watch.

"Is it time to start yet?" Marsh asked.

"Practically," Mr. Reedy said. "Tell me, Berger. Those reading lessons you asked me about. Did you ever do anything about them?"

Marsh's made-up, lined eyes widened. "What do you mean, *do* anything about them?"

"Are you taking lessons?"

The eyes narrowed. "Is Mr. Ellman out there?" Marsh asked.

"You have been taking lessons then?"

Marsh nodded.

"With this Mr. . . . Ellman, is it?"

Marsh nodded again.

"Is he a good teacher?"

Marsh felt like a little boy caught doing things with his pants down.

"Did my mother tell you about him?" he asked.

Mr. Reedy smiled. "I hope when you get on stage you're not going to do that," he said. "Answer questions with questions, I mean."

Marsh shrugged. "He's not really a teacher," he explained. "But he knows things."

"I'd like to meet him," Mr. Reedy said.

"Why?" Marsh asked. "There's nothing special about him. He just lives upstairs and a couple of times a week—"

"You go upstairs for lessons."

"Right."

"Just reading lessons? Or the memory too?"

"Both."

"Well, we have something in common then. We're both teachers of yours. After the quiz we'll get together and have a little talk."

Ellman's impulse was to return to his apartment, lock the door behind him and refuse to receive any of the Bergers. Instead he took a seat at the rear of the orchestra and began to phrase a new argument for Mr. Berger. "How could you expect me to succeed in an enterprise like this," he would say, "when I had neither the confidence nor the respect of the boy's parents themselves?" The very least he could have expected was a little courtesy on the part of Mrs. Berger. To be publicly dismissed like that was too much to be borne. Even if he had no other reason for ending the lessons, her actions would have made it impossible to continue.

The curtain went up, revealing about eight boys on the stage, four at each table. How claustrophobic the lessons seemed to Ellman now as he saw Marsh in perspective among his peers.

The principal of the school came out and made a brief speech expressing the pride the school took in all of its students and the special pride it took in those who had been chosen to be members of its quiz team. He then introduced Mr. Reedy.

Mr. Reedy was warmly applauded. In spite of the self-deprecating humor he brought to his description of the difficulties of organizing and coordinating a project like the quiz, he was clearly a man of no nonsense who knew his job and was respected by his students. Ellman was very impressed with him.

The teacher gave a brief outline of the way the quiz worked —the singles, doubles and team matches and the scoring system.

"You will notice," he said, "that there is a light bulb in the center of each table. Will the captain of each team please flash the switches."

The captains did so and both bulbs came on.

"We tried to install a buzzer like they use on the television program," Mr. Reedy explained, "but the only bell we could find that was loud enough to be heard throughout the auditorium was the one hooked into the fire alarm system. We experimented with that for a while until we found that every time one of the contestants pressed his button, another class would get up and march out of the school. We wouldn't have minded that so much if only the fire department hadn't been so nasty about it all."

Ellman envied Mr. Reedy the incredulously admiring looks of the contestants behind him and the admirable way he was handling the audience. He did not, however, join in the audience's laughter.

The next order of business was the introduction of the contestants. First there were the four "substitutes," who would appear on the television program only in the event that one or more of the regular team members were unable to appear. Last there were the four "team members," among whom Marsh was the third to be named. There were two team members and two substitutes on each side of the stage.

"And now, ladies and gentlemen, the quiz. First round, singles. Captain Gilson, have you chosen your lead-off man?"

"Dennis Kite."

"And Captain Berger?"

Marsh had chosen Jerry Tynan as his lead-off man.

The two lead-off men stepped forward and the quiz began.

They were quick, Ellman admitted. Quick and amazingly sharp. Questions and answers flew across the stage like tennis balls. Guesses and bluffs were shot down as fast as they were ventured. It all moved too quickly for thought and Ellman forgot his contempt for this reductio ad absurdum of knowledge in his attempt to move at the same pace as the quiz itself. His only breathing spaces came at a time when the questions were completely outside his ken, like mathematical questions about the cosine of x or the tangent of y.

Marsh was the last of his team to step forward for the singles round. It was captain versus captain at that point and Marsh started out with the disadvantage that his team was already ten points behind the other. Marsh and Gilson were two perfectly matched players. Every time Marsh was asked a question, Ellman held his breath waiting for the answer. Not once did this exercise place a strain on his respiratory system. Marsh was reassuringly right each time in a way that made Ellman's heart swell proudly. At the end of that round, Marsh's team was still ten points behind the other, but that was no fault of Marsh's. He had answered all of his questions correctly and so had his opponent.

Ellman wanted to nudge the lady next to him and say, "That's my Marshall. I coached him."

During the doubles round, Marsh's team gained a little ground. They were only six points behind the others when Marsh and Denny Lensman stepped forward to oppose Foster Gilson and Jerry Tynan.

It was a tense round, climaxing when Marsh was asked to name the general whose charge had turned the tide at Gettysburg.

Ellman held his breath longer than usual on that one.

At last Marsh ventured an answer. "Sheridan," he said.

Ellman did not release his breath.

"Pickett," said Mr. Reedy. "No points. Pickett's charge. Very famous."

There was a loud gasp, as though the entire audience, like Ellman, had been holding its breath. The gasp was followed by some self-conscious laughter and a brief flurry of excited applause. It was as though they had seen a trapeze artist fall into a net. Ellman was sorry Marsh had missed the question, of course, but the audience's reaction brought home to him the fact that everyone else was as aware as he of how perfect Marsh's performance had been up to that point.

"Pickett's charge," Ellman mused guiltily. "American history."

It was during the team round that the lights came into play. Only the first team to press its button was given an opportunity to answer the question. If their answer was correct, they gained ten points; if incorrect, they lost ten.

Marsh's side performed splendidly in the team round, although their glory was somewhat dimmed by the debate that arose over the light system. There were many times when both lights seemed to come on at the same time. Since Mr. Reedy was obliged to keep his eye on the paper from which he was reading the questions, the job of determining which team had pressed its button first fell to Mr. Dayson, a mathematics teacher. Many of the students in the audience were loud in their disagreement with Mr. Dayson's decisions.

Marsh's team lost by a score of 460 to 480, which served to calm those who were protesting that Mr. Dayson had favored Marsh's side.

"There will now be a brief intermission," Mr. Reedy announced. "We'll shuffle the teams up a bit and begin the second game in ten minutes."

Ellman went into the lobby for the intermission and spent most of his time leaning forward against the wall and listening to a man nearby explain to his friends how easy it would have been to rig both lights on the same circuit.

"That way they could have set it so that only one light could come on at a time," he explained. "Whichever team pressed its button first, that would be the only one whose light came on. There'd be no question about it."

Ellman looked down the hallway to see if Mrs. Berger and

her friends had come out for the intermission. Much to his surprise, he saw Marsh approaching.

"Marshall!" he said, extending his hand. "Congratulations."

Marsh looked uncomfortably self-conscious.

"I came out to find you," he said.

"Your mother told me you heard from City College," Ellman said. "Congratulations."

"Thank you," Marsh said. "Look, I can't talk now. I have to get backstage. With all this gook on my face, I must look like some kind of a freak."

"It's not as noticeable as—"

"After the show, could you stay around awhile? One of my teachers wants to meet you. Mr. Reedy."

"The one who's moderating the quiz? What does he want to meet me for?"

"I told him about the lessons. It slipped out really. Anyway, he says he wants to meet you. He even reminded me about it just now. In fact, he's the one who sent me out here to make sure you don't leave before he has a chance to see you."

Ellman did not know whether to be pleased or anxious. He tried to find a clue in Marsh's face, but Marsh was glancing around him.

"Do you know where my mother is?" he asked.

"I think she's sitting on the other side of the auditorium with some friends."

"Oh, well, I'll see her after. I better get back now while they choose up teams for the next game. I'll see you later."

"Where?" was all Ellman had time to ask.

"Right here, I guess," Marsh said.

Some of the people nearby, recognizing Marsh as he pushed his way through the crowd, glanced from him to Ellman in an inquisitive way, as if trying to determine the relationship between them. One woman smiled at Ellman and said, "He's very good. Is he your grandson?"

"No," Ellman said, smiling back at her. "Just a friend."

During the second game Ellman's attention was divided between following what was going on onstage and worrying about what it was that Mr. Reedy wanted to say to him. It was dangerous and foolish to expect admiration from him, and yet the teacher could hardly be about to call Ellman to task for doing Marsh any harm. He had not done him any harm. On the contrary, the proof of Ellman's good work was being given on the stage that very day; and if that was not enough, there was the letter from City College. That alone was all the justification Ellman needed. It was ridiculous and presumptuous for this teacher, or any teacher, to think of calling Ellman to account.

Fortunately, Ellman's mind was taken off such speculations by the antics of both sides in the team round, which had some of the earmarks of slapstick comedy about it.

During the intermission they had decided to dispense with the lights altogether. The procedure now called for any boy who thought he knew the answer to leap to his feet, it being felt that it would be easier to determine which boy had popped up first than to decide which light went on first.

Clearly there was nothing timid about any of the team members. They soon took on the aspect of so many jack-in-the-boxes. There was great scraping of wood when the round began, as each contestant moved his chair backward in order to get his legs out from under the table. A couple of times the tables were nearly upset and several times the contestants, in their eagerness to rise to the challenge, knocked their chairs down behind them. One chair in particular got several laughs. It was a folding chair and each time it hit the ground it slowly folded itself closed as if deciding that it wanted no more of such undignified proceedings.

Marsh was not captain during the second game but the team he was on won. The audience filed out of the auditorium in a satisfied, contented mood.

The departing crowd had thinned out somewhat by the time Marsh, shorn of his makeup, joined Ellman in the lobby. Mrs. Berger was already with him and she was encouraging him to move on almost before Ellman had finished congratulating him on his success.

"I want to go straight to your Aunt Rona's," Mrs. Berger said, "to tell her you got accepted."

"We have to wait awhile first," Marsh said. "Mr. Reedy wants to meet Mr. Ellman."

Mrs. Berger's face fell. "What for?" she asked.

"How do I know what for? He just wants to meet him."

Ellman too would have liked to know why the teacher wanted to meet him.

"What did he say when you told him about the lessons?" he asked Marsh.

"Nothing much," Marsh answered evasively.

Before Ellman could question him any further, Marsh's voice cracked into a "There he is" as he pointed to the approaching Mr. Reedy.

"So you're Marsh's tutor," Mr. Reedy said warmly as he was introduced to Ellman.

Confronted now by Marsh's licensed-by-law and upheld-by-tradition teacher, the tutor suddenly felt foolish and inadequate. Mr. Reedy was somehow too neat, too confident, too well-focused to please Ellman. In his presence Ellman felt like a fuzzy amateur about to be questioned by a sharp professional. He glanced quickly toward the door as if to make sure his line of escape was open.

"I try to help a little," he said.

"Marsh hasn't told me very much about it," Mr. Reedy said. "What subjects do you help him in?"

"English and American history," Mrs. Berger put in. "It's just once or twice a week. He helps Marsh with his homework."

Ellman would have been pleased to impose this deception on the teacher. He looked at Marsh to see if the boy would agree to this. Marsh was frowning, but Ellman could not be sure if the source of his discomfort lay in his mother's lie or in the necessity of exposing the truth to his teacher.

Mr. Reedy was saying in the gentlest possible way that he thought he had heard something somewhere about some reading and memory exercises.

"I help him a little bit with his reading," Ellman said. "I've also taught him a few memory tricks."

"Tricks?" There was a slight twinkle in his eyes as Mr. Reedy pronounced the word.

Ellman felt a cold wind blowing on him, forcing everything in him to stiffen in place. It was the kind of feeling he had not had since he was a boy. Mr. Reedy was Authority. Better educated and surer of itself than Ellman could ever be, that Authority was now calling on Julius Ellman to account for himself.

"I th-think of myself m-more as a h-helper than as a t-teacher," Ellman said. He did not actually stutter as he spoke the words. Rather, he held on to the first consonant for a long while, refusing to release the word until the first sound of it was well-shaped in his mouth. The result was that there were long pauses between the words, as if he were not really speaking, but staggering like a drunkard from one phrase to another.

"It's a kind of game," Mrs. Berger said. "Like the quiz. Marsh reads a book and they ask questions about it."

Ellman looked again toward the exit.

Marsh cleared his throat so loudly that everyone, including

Ellman, suddenly looked his way. Marsh's gaze, however, was firmly fixed on Mr. Reedy.

"Mr. Ellman teaches me reading, comprehension and memory," he said. "I study with him three nights a week, although we may cut it down to one soon."

"I'm not a speed reader myself," Mr. Ready said to Ellman. "I've often envied people who could do it, though. Did you study it for long?"

Ellman, hung up on a *p*, took a long while to get out the word. "Privately."

"Memory too?"

"I have s-several b-books on the s-subject."

"As far as memory is concerned," Marsh said loudly, "we've concentrated on specifics. Analysis of documents in terms of key words linked in a chain, geography in terms of miniature spacial division, history in terms of cause-and-effect sequence set against a visual-key background."

For once Mrs. Berger had nothing to say. She looked from Marsh to Ellman with a countenance that clearly reflected the dawning of a new idea in her mind. For the first time it was brought home to her that Marsh was getting something out of his relationship with Ellman after all.

Ellman had no idea where Marsh had got the jargon about "miniature spacial divisions" and "visual-key backgrounds." Neither of these phrases was in any of Ellman's books. Possibly Marsh had improvised them on the spot. All Ellman could be certain of was that Marsh was trying to speak for him because it was so painfully clear that Ellman could not speak for himself.

The only one who was not impressed by Marsh's speech was Mr. Reedy.

"I haven't the slightest idea what any of that means," he said, smiling. "It sounds much too complicated for me."

Marsh started to explain the analysis of the Constitution but

Mr. Reedy cut him off by asking Ellman how he found time for such things. "It must take up nearly all your spare time."

"All my t-time is s-spare," Ellman explained. "I'm r-retired."

"I see," Mr. Reedy replied. "You were a teacher?"

"N-no," Mr. Ellman said. "I was w-with the p-post office." Ellman closed his eyes. "My b-brother was a v-violinist." That was another habit he had forgotten. Each time he told someone that he worked for the post office, he found himself obliged to add, as if the family honor depended on it, that his brother was a violinist.

"What school did you go to?"

"City schools."

"No. I mean what college?"

Ellman was tempted to lie, but he resisted the temptation. Once he had wanted to tell Marsh the truth, to start off on a clean slate. Let him hear the truth now, Ellman thought, and end it once and for all.

"I n-n-never w-went to c-c-c-college," he said. "W-we c-couldn't af-ford it."

"You went to high school, though?"

"N-no."

Mr. Reedy's expression did not change. "It must have been difficult for you," he said lightly.

It was clearly a blow to Marsh and it intensified the quandary Mrs. Berger found herself in. She had just accepted the fact that Ellman had been of some professional help to Marsh and now she found that his help had not been professional at all.

"You told my husband you went to college," she protested. "He said you were an educated man."

Ellman said nothing.

"What difference does it make anyway?" Marsh said. "The proof of the pudding is in the eating, isn't it?"

"Not if it's predigested," Mr. Reedy said thoughtfully.

Marsh frowned, not understanding what Mr. Reedy meant.

Mr. Reedy put out his hand to Ellman. "It's been nice meeting you," he said. "I have to be getting on now."

Ellman shook his hand limply.

"You have a fine boy there, Mrs. Berger. I expect great things from him in the quiz. Marsh, I'll see you on Monday."

"We have to get to Aunt Rona's," Mrs. Berger said after Mr. Reedy had departed.

"You coming?" Marsh asked Ellman. "My aunt lives only a couple of blocks from us. It's the same bus ride."

"I won't be taking the bus," Ellman said slowly. "I'm taking the subway. I have to go to my friend Callahan's. I promised him."

Marsh tried, but was unable to get the old man to look him in the eyes. "Okay," he said. "We'll see you later then."

"Yes," Ellman said. "Good-bye."

Chapter 18

Ellman had lied about the promise to Callahan but since he had told Marsh and his mother that he was taking the subway, he began to walk in that direction. When he reached the corner, he shrugged and walked down into the station. There he purchased a token, went on to the platform and stood with the crowd waiting for the uptown train.

Several students from Marsh's school were waiting there also. They were all carrying canvas bags, a couple of which had the names of airlines printed on them. As Ellman approached, one of the boys took a seat and proceeded to change from the shoes he was wearing into a pair of sneakers that he fished out of his bag.

Ellman walked to the edge of the platform and made a pretense of looking to see if the train was coming. *What do I care if the train comes or not?* Ellman thought. *I have no place to go anyway.*

Behind him, the boys were laughing and joking, cracking each other up by quoting lines from a television commercial.

"Do you have a foot-care problem?" one asked.

"Changing your socks is not always the answer," said another. "The problem may lie with *you.*"

The boys' attempts at wit made Ellman tired. He walked along the platform, trying to recall something he had read about the repetition of advertising slogans out of context being a poor substitute for wit, but he could not remember the gist of the argument. Something about the frame of reference changing from the "world of natural phenomena and human experience to a fantasy world created by merchants with products to sell."

Ellman looked back at the boys. Some of them had got hold of a shoe and were throwing it back and forth to each other, amid protestations that none of them wanted to hold the "stinking thing." The shoe's owner, meanwhile, gave up his efforts to retrieve it and sat down again. When the others threatened to throw the shoe down on the track, however, he got up once more and the game resumed.

A middle-aged woman, passing the boys, was nearly hit with the shoe. She stopped to remonstrate.

"This is no place to play games like that," she said. "Save that for outside. It's dangerous in a place like this."

"We're just fooling around," one of the boys said.

"Fool around someplace else," the woman answered, walking on in a huff. "Not in a subway station."

"Kids!" a man near Ellman said. "They don't have any respect anymore."

"Why should they have respect?" Ellman said. "What do we show them that deserves respect?"

The man, who was neatly dressed in a gray suit similar to the one Mr. Reedy had worn, had clearly not expected any answer. He turned away, muttered, "Whatever you say," and made an elaborate show of looking for the train.

"What does it matter what I say?" Ellman said. "I have no degree."

A downtown train pulled in on the other side of the station. Under the blanket of noise it provided, Ellman began mumbling to himself.

"Marshall did everything he could to help me even while I

was standing there stuttering like a fool," he said. "That's all the qualifications and all the justification and all the success I need."

The man in the gray suit could not possibly hear what Ellman was saying, but he noticed the lips moving.

"Better to have knowledge predigested than never digested at all," Ellman said. He was still addressing the gray suit directly, and it amused him that the man made a polite pretense of trying to understand what he was saying.

"It doesn't matter now," Ellman said. "It's all behind me anyway."

The man looked behind Ellman and smiled.

As the downtown local pulled out of the station, the uptown train began to pull in. The man in the gray suit made a gesture of salute to Ellman and moved off down the platform, as if he wanted a seat in one of the rear cars. The boys, however, took hold of their bags and began to move in Ellman's direction. He got into the same car they did.

"Poor fellow," Ellman said, thinking of the gray suit as the train pulled out. "He thinks I'm losing control, that I don't know what I'm doing." He looked down at the other end of the car, where the boys seemed to be improvising a variation of tag. "But I do know what I'm doing," he said. "I'm having a good time." His eyes swept a row of posters lining the car and came to rest on a cigarette advertisement.

"Like a free man should," he added, and laughed at his own joke.

It was lecturing the boys on the wisdom of studying without books and asking the man who told him to leave them alone what college he had gone to. It was sitting next to a woman on a park bench at the end of the subway line and gently telling her that it really didn't matter if one's dreams did not work out when one was old, that the important thing was to hold on to the dream because that was what kept you young. And it was laughing at the way the woman agreed with him, as though she thought he really believed what he was saying.

It was finding himself downtown again because he remembered that he wanted to see Callahan, and it was walking into a bookstore and asking the clerk how many he had actually read of the books he had in stock and how long it took him to read each one and how much he would charge to have them destroyed by a teacher of reading, even though he had no qualifications. It was walking down the street declaring that knowledge was the province of all, that maps drew artificial boundaries around this province and that one could memorize the map by analyzing it in terms of one's own living room.

It was not finding Callahan at home and being relieved at not finding Callahan at home because now the game could go on. It was reciting Callahan's Sputnik poem to the world at large.

> "Listen, my children, and you shall hear
> The beep-beep-beep from the stratosphere."

> "What year was the first satellite launched?"

> "On the fourth of October in fifty-seven
> Sputnik went to its place in heaven."

It was asking a young man in a delicatessen if he stuttered and telling him that the only way to get over it was to get over it and to watch out because you might think you're over it, only you're not. It was explaining to the young man that it was dreams that kept you from being honest and free. "They make you old before your time. That's why the boys in the subway couldn't act their age. They didn't have imagination enough to be dreamers. All they could do was quote commercials."

It was explaining to the woman outside the delicatessen that even though dreams made you old before your time, they left you young after it.

It was riding the subway again, walking through the cars looking for students, finding none and telling the conductor that the subway system was potentially the greatest university the city had. It was finding that the conductor knew every station from Flatbush Avenue to White Plains and telling him that that was enough knowledge to build an encyclopedia on.

"Suppose I were to tell you you could become an expert in any field you chose just by letting me populate the subway stations for you? Hang posters and show movies and stage battles. But all in the mind. *Your* mind."

It was finding himself lost in Brooklyn in the dark and not caring that he was lost because there was more sky to be seen in Brooklyn than there was in Manhattan and because the sky was full of cold stars and Ellman felt at home among them.

It was all this that Ellman remembered when he found himself explaining to a policeman that he knew who he was and could produce identification but that he needed directions because he had taken the wrong train and was lost.

"As soon as the other kids got back from school," Aunt Rona said, "she announced she was feeling better. I told her if she was too sick to go to school, she was too sick to go out and play. Not that she was faking. She did have a temperature this morning."

Aunt Rona had been presented with the letter from City College as soon as they arrived at her house and had read it and congratulated Marsh while Mrs. Berger was still taking her coat off. Now Marsh was anxious to get out of her house and be on his way home.

"I was really looking forward to going to your quiz program this afternoon too," she explained, concluding the recital of her daughter's illness.

"Maybe it's just as well you didn't go," Mrs. Berger said.

Aunt Rona looked shocked.

"Don't get me wrong, the quiz part was all right," Mrs.

Berger explained. "But after the quiz. That Mr. Ellman I was telling you about. I could have died."

"I got a date with Donna tonight," Marsh said. "I want to go home first and get some reading and homework out of the way."

"Doing your homework on a Friday afternoon?" Aunt Rona said. "I don't even know my kids have homework on weekends until Sunday night. As soon as I tell them it's time to go to bed, that's when they remember they have homework."

"He doesn't have to do homework," Mrs. Berger said. "The principal announced this afternoon that the people in the quiz are all excused from it. He just doesn't want to hear me say anything about his precious Ellman."

"I *want* to do the homework," Marsh explained. "I don't *have* to do it, but if I let it slide because of the quiz, I might fall behind. I still have final examinations to take this year."

"Well, he's going to hear a lot more about Ellman," Mrs. Berger continued. "Him and his father both. I don't care what either of them says. That's all over and done with. You're not going up to him anymore and that's final."

"I better get at that homework," Marsh said. With a polite good-bye to his Aunt Rona, he left.

"I'll be home in half an hour," his mother called after him. "I have to start getting supper ready."

By the time her husband arrived home that night, Mrs. Berger had blown much of the chaff from her arguments. What was left was as irreducible and irrefutable as the future course it led to was inevitable.

Ellman had not told them that he had not gone to college. Therefore he was a liar. Mrs. Berger had no intention of letting her son be taught by liars.

Ellman had confessed that he had no personal experience of the things he was supposed to be teaching Marsh. Mrs. Berger had no intention of letting her son be taught by a phony who didn't know what he was doing.

Finally, Ellman *knew* he had no business teaching. He had not even been able to look Mr. Reedy in the eye, but had stuttered and sputtered and ended up letting Marsh do most of the talking for him. Mrs. Berger had no intention of letting her son be taught by anybody who didn't even have guts enough to stand up for himself.

"It's Marsh that should be teaching *him* and not the other way around."

When Mr. Berger received confirmation from Marsh of the afternoon's events, he was visibly shaken. The only defense he offered was, "Well, we didn't *ask* him if he ever went to college, did we?"

"*You* didn't," his wife said. "Anyway, he's crazy. If he went to ten colleges, he'd still be crazy. We're just lucky we found out about it when we did."

"He's not crazy," Marsh said.

"No, he's not crazy," Mrs. Berger said. "He just likes to talk to himself because he can't talk to anybody else without sounding like a moron. He likes to teach things that he never studied himself."

"It's not important whether he studied them himself or not," Marsh said.

"He never even went to high school!" Mrs. Berger said. "Do you realize right now you got more education than he ever had?"

Mr. Berger forced a rueful laugh. "He's got more education than we had too, when you come down to it."

Mrs. Berger pinned her husband to the wall with a glare.

"It's not the same thing," she said. "We're his parents. You with your wisecracks; whose side are you on anyway?"

"Mr. Reedy didn't say there was anything wrong with my working with Ellman," Marsh pointed out.

"I know what Mr. Reedy said," Mrs. Berger answered. "He said he'd talk to you on Monday. And I saw the way he looked at you when he said it. I know what he's going to tell you. You've been on very dangerous ground and he's going to tell you to stop this Ellman stuff right away. And before he tells you that, you're going to tell him that you *have* stopped it."

"Oh, no I'm not," Marsh said.

There was a moment of absolute silence around the dinner table. It was the first time Marsh had ever declared himself diametrically opposed to his mother, and it took a moment for the shock waves to pass.

"I don't mean it disrespectfully," Marsh said. "But the only one who can judge whether Ellman has been good or bad for me is me. I say he's been good and I'm going to go on with the lessons."

They had been sitting in the kitchen. Marsh now rose from the table and announced that he had to start getting ready for his date that night.

"I'll tell you something funny," he said, turning to his parents once more. "Ellman wanted to end the lessons himself. He said he was getting too old and tired. Now, with you and Mr. Reedy both against him, he has an even better excuse for quitting. But I'm not going to let him quit. And I don't care what Reedy or anybody else thinks."

"Over my dead body," said Mrs. Berger, rising angrily from the table and following Marsh into the living room.

"I'm sorry," Marsh said. "That's the way it is."

"Now hold on just a minute, the both of you!" Mr. Berger too rose from the table and followed the others into the living room. "Marsh, sit down. I want to talk to you."

"I have to get ready—"

"It won't take a minute. Sit down."

"It's about time you opened your mouth," Mrs. Berger said.

Mr. Berger and his son sat facing one another on the couch.

Marsh's expression was one of sullen determination. Mr. Berger's was equally determined, but tinged with sadness.

"I know how you feel, Marsh," he said. "Because I was all for the Ellman thing too. If anybody ought to look ridiculous at the way things turned out, it ought to be me. The whole thing was my idea in the first place."

"It was a *good* idea," Marsh insisted.

"It seemed a good idea at the time," Mr. Berger said. "But it wasn't."

"I told you that all along," Mrs. Berger said.

"You told me he was a crazy old man," Mr. Berger said. "What good is that? Everybody you don't like is crazy. You're very big on qualifications now but did you say one word about them then? Did you say, 'Ask him what college he went to, what his major is'? No. All you said was 'He's a crazy old man.' You're still saying the same thing."

"And I'll go on saying it," Mrs. Berger said. "Because it's true."

Mr. Berger spoke to Marsh again.

"I should have asked him all those things," he said. "Instead, you know what I did?"

Mr. Berger got to his feet, paced about the living room and then pointed to the ceiling.

"I went upstairs," he said. "I went to that apartment with my hat in my hand and I practically told that guy the whole story of my life. I told him about the ambition I used to have. I must have made a damned fool of myself telling him how I couldn't afford to go to college but I wanted you to have it better than I did. He had plenty of opportunity to be just as level with me as I was with him, but no, he didn't say a damned word. Just 'Send him up. We'll start the lessons.'"

"But he was right," Marsh said. "Even if he didn't—"

"Oh, I'm not blaming him," Mr. Berger said. "I asked him for help and in his own way he tried to give it. But what I'm saying is this—that if I knew then what I know now I'd never have let things go this far."

"You think it ought to stop." It was a statement rather than a question.

"I *know* it ought to stop. And it's going to."

"But the memory and the reading. Remember, you're the one who started me on that."

"I made a mistake. I admit it."

"He memorized a whole newspaper. You kept raving about it."

"It was a good trick. If your Mr. Reedy wanted to do tricks like that, I'm sure he could learn them. But you don't get an education by doing tricks. Mr. Reedy's got the kind of qualifications Ellman *ought* to have. Should have had if he was going to set himself up for a teacher. Your mother was right about one thing—you get what you pay for. So if you want a teacher, get a *teacher*, and don't look for one in a bargain basement."

Marsh shook his head.

"You don't understand," he said.

"I understand one thing," Mr. Berger said, pointing to the ceiling once more. "You've seen the last of Ellman. I'm going to talk to him and I'm going to tell him the lessons are over. And if *I* tell him they're over, it doesn't matter what *you* tell him."

When Ellman woke up Saturday morning, his wanderings of the night before were still quite vivid in his mind. He knew that it was only by luck that he had not ended the night by being carted off to Bellevue for observation. His behavior had been that of a drunkard and, as he sat at the edge of the bed, he was strangely bothered by the fact that he had no hangover. A hangover would have been punishment and expiation for his foolishness, allowing him to forget it.

"The worst is past," he told himself. "The mistake lay not

in celebrating the lifting of the burden, but in undertaking to carry it in the first place."

He made himself a pot of coffee and some toast and fried two eggs. When breakfast was finished, he put his plate into the sink and ran water over it. Then he went into the living room, drew several books from the shelf and piled them on the table. After that he sat in an armchair and waited. It was not until late afternoon that the knock came at the door.

It was Mr. Berger.

"I came up last night but you weren't here," he said.

Ellman invited him in.

One glance at Mr. Berger's face told Ellman that he had heard all about the incident at the school the day before. For an instant he felt chagrined. Then the calm returned.

Mr. Berger looked distastefully at the bookshelf.

"I guess you know what I've come for," he said.

"*Tell* me," Ellman answered.

"The lessons," Mr. Berger said. "They're over."

"Yes, I know. I told Marshall the other day I intended to end them. He didn't seem to believe me."

The corners of Mr. Berger's mouth curled downward in an expression of disgust.

"If that's supposed to make me think that that business with the teacher yesterday was all an act, you can just forget it."

"I went to the school yesterday in hopes of finding you there. I wanted to tell you I couldn't go on with the lessons."

Mr. Berger shrugged. "All right," he said. "As long as you and I both understand that it's all over, there's no point in talking about it, is there?"

He began to walk to the door.

"Wait a minute," Ellman said. "I have some books here. I want Marshall to have them."

"He doesn't need them," Mr. Berger said. "And I don't want them."

"Even if I can't do any more for Marshall," Ellman said, "these books can."

"We don't want anything from you," Berger said.

Once more Mr. Berger moved to the doorway and once more Ellman called him to stop.

"Give me some credit," he said. "I did help Marshall a little. Now I'm asking you to help me. I want to get rid of these books. I don't want them around the house anymore. They're part of something I'm finished with."

"So throw them out."

"I can't," Ellman said. "Not when I know they can be of some use to somebody. There's nothing to stop you from throwing them out if you want, though. All I'm asking is that you take them away with you."

Silently Mr. Berger put out his hands. Ellman took the pile of books from the table and handed them over. The volume on top was entitled *The Ten Keys to Magic Memory*. From the curious glance Mr. Berger gave it, Ellman knew it would be some time before the books found their way into the trashcan.

That night Callahan telephoned him. In simple, straightforward terms, Ellman told him about the interview with Marsh's teacher and his talk with Mr. Berger. He made no mention, however, of his wandering about the city the night before.

"Do you want me to come over?" Callahan said. "We can talk."

"No," Ellman answered. "I assure you I'm all right."

"Maybe it's just as well you're free now," Callahan said at length. "I didn't want to mention it before while you had your mind on the other thing, but I've been thinking a lot lately about that old mnemonic poem idea we were working on. To tell the truth, I don't think we'll ever get four lines as tightly knit as we wanted, but I was thinking that if we could tie the poem into some one specific event and weave in the names of all the people and things involved in that event, we'd really have a format we could build on. What do you think?"

Ellman was ninety percent sure that this was just a device on Callahan's part to give him something besides Marsh to think about.

"Do you know how to play pinochle?" he asked.

"Sure," Callahan said. "Why?"

"I'll work on the mnemonic if you want me to," Ellman siad, "but only on the condition that you teach me how to play pinochle. Agreed?"

Callahan laughed into the phone.

"Agreed," he said.

Chapter 19

Every night that week, Callahan telephoned to be sure Ellman was all right and every night Ellman told him he was busy working on the mnemonic.

"Did you go out today?" Callahan asked.

"No. Not today. I've been busy."

"It's not good to stay cooped up in the house all the time. You should get out, even if it's just for a walk around the block. As my father used to say, if you'll pardon the expression, you have to get out and blow the stink off you."

A couple of times Callahan asked about Marsh, but Ellman said he had not seen or heard from him.

"That's the part I don't get," Callahan said. "You'd think he'd at least have come up to say thank you or good-bye. Something at least."

Ellman would hear nothing against Marsh.

"His parents wouldn't like it," he said.

"Don't kid yourself," Callahan said. "It never even occurred to him. He got his and that's the end of it as far as he's concerned. And you won't really be over it until you accept that."

On Thursday evening Ellman went out to the grocery for some milk. When he was halfway down the block, he saw Mr. Berger approaching.

Recognizing Ellman, Mr. Berger stopped for a moment,

gave him an appraising glance and said, "I guess you got your way after all."

Ellman had no idea what he was talking about.

On Saturday morning, Callahan called and told Ellman he wanted to see him at his house.

"What for?" Ellman asked.

"So you'll get out of *your* house," he said. "Besides, it's time for your first pinochle lesson. No kidding, you're coming over here today if I have to go over there and drag you."

Ellman went to Callahan's room.

They talked about the mnemonic for a while and then Callahan pulled out a brand-new pinochle deck with the seal still unbroken. After a few hands, Callahan turned the television set on.

"Deal again," he told Ellman while he was adjusting the set.

There was a war movie on. Callahan focused the picture and turned the volume off. Then he went back to the cards.

"It's on the right channel," he said. "This way we'll be sure to see the quiz when it starts."

"The quiz?" Ellman repeated.

"Today's the day Marshall is on, isn't it? You don't want to miss that?"

Ellman concentrated on arranging his cards.

"It still hurts, doesn't it?" Callahan said. "Well, take it from an expert—it's going to go on hurting until you talk about it."

Ellman did not raise his eyes from his cards.

"It doesn't hurt," he said.

"Don't give me that."

"It hurt the first night, but it hasn't hurt since," Ellman said. "I wasted a lot of years on foolishness. I can't afford to waste more time sitting around being hurt."

"It'd be nice if things worked out that way," Callahan said. "But they don't. They never have."

After another two hands of pinochle, the quiz came on and they put the cards aside to watch it.

"So that's what Marshall looks like," Callahan said. "He's a nice-looking kid, I'll give him that."

Marsh's face looked thinner and stronger on television than it did in person.

As the first order of business, the moderator introduced each member of the team and asked them a little bit about themselves. Ellman decided that it would be interesting to hear what Marsh's voice would sound like over the television.

"My name is Marshall Berger," he said, "and I'm a senior." Then, in response to a question from the moderator, he said, "I'm going to enter City College in the fall and I plan to become a teacher."

The moderator said something about that being a very commendable ambition, but his comment was lost in Callahan's yell. "A teacher! I thought you said he was going to be an engineer."

Ellman wished that the moderator had been as surprised by Marsh's announcement as he was—surprised enough, at any rate, to ask how, when and why he had come by this ambition. But the moderator had already passed on to the next contestant.

Callahan was still staring at Ellman.

"Don't look at me," Ellman said. "I didn't know anything about it. But in answer to your earlier question—no, it doesn't hurt at all anymore. Not at all."

71 72 73 74 75 10 9 8 7 6 5 4 3 2 1